THE LEGACY SERIES

The Path of Totality
Marie Zhuikov

Shocker in Gloomtown
Dan Libman

The Continental Divide
Bob Johnson

The Three Devils and Other Stories
William Luvaas

The Correct Response
Manfred Gabriel

Welcome Back to the World: A Novella & Stories
Rob Davidson

Greyhound Cowboy and Other Stories
Ken Post

Close Call
Kim Suhr

The Waterman
Gary Schanbacher

Signs of the Imminent Apocalypse and Other Stories
Heidi Bell

What We Might Become
Sara Reish Desmond

The Silver State Stories
Michael Darcher

An Instinct for Movement
Michael Mattes

"For the characters in Michael Keefe's *Western Terminus*, living in the present offers a kind of peace—not borne from naïveté, but hard-won. A peace gained by examining the past as well as their physical place, seeing both the beauty and filth in reality. You can go home again, these vivid and startling stories say, but only after you've had a historical or personal reckoning."

—RACHEL KING
author of *Bratwurst Haven: Stories*
winner of the Colorado Book Award

"*Western Terminus* couldn't be a more perfect title for this collection of stories about men and women travelling through their past lives, and their present circumstances, with the history and knowledge of how their homelands at the edge of a particular world shaped everything. Michael Keefe has brought me back to these places with his prickly love for the outskirts, the missed love, and stubborn loyalty to people even when they might not deserve us. I loved reading these stories!"

—SUSAN STRAIGHT
National Book Award finalist
author of *Mecca*

"In Michael Keefe's searching collection, *Western Terminus*, characters fling themselves far into their personal abysses until gravity ultimately reasserts itself. I found myself rooting for each surprising, gorgeous disaster. Mesmerizing and tightly woven, these beautiful stories inspire as much as they enlighten."

—ERIKA KROUSE
author of *Save Me, Stranger*

WESTERN TERMINUS

stories and a novella

MICHAEL KEEFE

CORNERSTONE PRESS
UNIVERSITY OF WISCONSIN-STEVENS POINT

Cornerstone Press, Stevens Point, Wisconsin 54481
Copyright © 2025 Michael Keefe
www.uwsp.edu/cornerstone

Printed in the United States of America by
Point Print and Design Studio, Stevens Point, Wisconsin

Library of Congress Control Number: 2025943465
ISBN: 978-1-968148-08-9

This is a work of fiction. Names, characters, businesses, places, events, and incidents are either the products of the author's imagination or used in a fictitious manner. Any resemblance to actual persons, living or dead, or actual events is purely coincidental.

Cornerstone Press titles are produced in courses and internships offered by the Department of English at the University of Wisconsin–Stevens Point.

DIRECTOR & PUBLISHER
Dr. Ross K. Tangedal

EXECUTIVE EDITORS
Jeff Snowbarger, Freesia McKee

EDITORIAL DIRECTOR
Brett Hill

SENIOR EDITORS
Paige Biever, Eva Nielsen, Reilly Crous

PRESS STAFF
Lilly Kulbeck, Ryleigh Miller, Leo Poskozim, Sam Zajkowski, Samantha Bjork, Sophie McPherson, Madison Schultz, Autumn Vine

For Gaynl

Contents

A System of Dares

I'm on the phone with Janey Hopstetter when Dad erupts into a coughing fit. He's in the living room, and I'm out on the back porch, but his phlegmy bark is so damn loud I have to cover up my phone until the racket dies down. Mom is shriveling away in hospice, and it sounds like Dad isn't far behind. But what am I supposed to do? I can't afford a live-in nurse, and I'm sure as hell not driving down from Los Angeles every weekend just to make sure he's swallowing his pills. Besides, Dad and I have always enjoyed what my wife likes to call a "laissez-faire dynamic." LeeAnn's in real estate, but she was a Psych major in college, which apparently qualifies her to diagnose everyone she meets. Here's her assessment of my relationship with our son, Tyler: "Not super dysfunctional." Well, the kid's only twelve—there's still time for me to screw him up worse.

I put the phone back up to my ear and catch Janey mid-sentence. She must've been talking all through Dad's coughing fit. "No kidding," I say because it sounds like she's telling that kind of story. So-and-so has troubled kids, or got fired from wherever, or needs some kind of medical procedure. The details fail to arouse my curiosity. But the thought of getting into the pants of my high school crush? Well, no one's aroused that part of me in a very long time. So I encourage her babbling with little interjections—an "mm-hm" here and an "oh, really?" there. LeeAnne would know that I'm only pretending to listen, but my wife's not on the phone right now. "Janey," I say. "How about I pick you up at seven? We'll catch up more over a couple of steaks."

"Mmm, sounds great." She says, and I can almost feel the warmth of her breath against my cheek.

I never had my chance with Janey back in the day. She and Beau Reynolds started going out sophomore year of high school, then got married not long after graduation. Beau was always a total prick to me. The thought of fucking his ex-wife really sweetens the deal. My voice goes low and gravelly. Intimate. "See you then."

The evening is balmy and clear. I linger on the porch and watch the sun dip down between a pair of eucalyptus trees. In the neighbor's orange grove, green waxy leaves shine gold. A pink glow settles on the wide rolling scrubland beyond. This is the part of home I always miss: a world that's open and alive.

When I come back inside, Dad's asleep in the Barcalounger. I pry the smoldering cigarette from his yellowed fingers. And maybe I'm reverting back to my teenage years because I'm tempted to gulp down the watery dregs of his Jack and Coke. Then I notice the spittle on his cracked lips and I remember the slimy gunk sputtering up from his lungs. I carry his glass to the kitchen sink and fix myself a whiskey neat. Because I'm the adult now, right? At forty-one, having a dead parent wouldn't be considered a tragedy. In truth, Mom's death will come as a relief. The end of suffering. Hers, and ours.

I stand in the kitchen—the old warmth and bustle of decades past now bled from the air. In the next room, my father's ragged snores come in jumps and stops. It's too early to leave for Janey's, so I tip another splash of whiskey into my glass. The clock on the microwave blinks once every second. I drink and watch time flicker by.

IT'S WHEN I PULL the car keys out of my pocket that I notice my wedding ring. I might've hinted to Janey that I'm divorced. It's more like LeeAnn and I are separated. We still live together, but that's only because L.A. is too damn expensive to pay rent on two places. LeeAnn hasn't been reeling in the big commissions. And my list of clients—actors who once landed lead roles on sitcoms and soaps—are lucky to get commercials these days. Plus, there's Tyler's college tuition to save for. Mortgage, car payments, medical bills. Death by a thousand paper cuts.

I tug the ring off my finger. But my nerves are shot, and maybe I'm a little buzzed. The ring slips from my grasp and bounces underneath an unruly clump of geranium bushes. For the past six months, Mom's been too sick to keep her flower garden pruned. And Dad couldn't give a shit about nature—until a squirrel chews through the cable line. Anyway, I'll find the ring tomorrow morning. Unless a crow beats me to it. They're suckers for shiny crap. Maybe Mr. Crow will use my ring to propose to the future Mrs. Crow. I raise my flask to the trees and say a "mazel tov" to the Crows. Then I climb inside my old Beamer and roll down the dirt driveway of my childhood home.

It's when I make the turn toward Janey's side of town that I realize I haven't been out this way in years. The nighttime streets look unfamiliar, like patches of my memory are smudged-out. I'm squinting at a street sign when a wall of hedges whirs up out of the void. I swerve and stomp the breaks. My tires skid to a stop, inches away from an avocado tree in someone's front yard. Porch lights snap on, and I back out in a hurry.

I found a few pictures of Janey Hopstetter online. She still has curves in all the right places. I've tried to keep myself fit, too. But, even when I'm out for a jog, my blood runs stagnant in my veins. I need motion. Contact. The hard slap of flesh and nerve.

My car needs gas, and the Chevron up ahead is lit up bright. With no other cars in sight, the station looks forlorn. I pull up to the pump, get out, and swipe my credit card. When the little readout says I'm authorized, I let out a long breath. It feels like I've been holding that same breath for weeks now. Years, maybe.

I jam the nozzle into place and squeeze the trigger. That's when I spot him through the big plate glass window: Beau Reynolds. He's wearing oil-stained coveralls, his hairline's crawled back, and his gut's gone to flab since his days on the varsity wrestling team. But I recognize the idiot frown on his Neanderthal brow. A cordless phone is pressed against his ear and he's staring right back at me. What's the story, Beau? Did you call up your asshole buddies the second I pulled in? Jake Milligan and Corey Briggs. Beau and those dickheads tortured me for years.

I've only put a few gallons in the tank, but that'll take me where I need to go. I tap the nozzle against the fuel pipe—just like jiggling away those last drops of piss—and screw the gas cap back on.

"Hey, Craig."

Beau's voice rattles my spine, and I spurt gasoline on my shoe. Great. Now, when I pick up Janey, I'm going to smell like her ex-husband.

I turn to face him. "Shit, Beau. Thanks a lot."

"Oh, man." He winces at my feet. "Sorry."

My skin prickles and my chest tightens up. All the old rage starts spinning around my head. "You know what, Beau? Fuck you guys."

"Whoa." Beau raises his hands, like I'm after his wallet instead of his wife. "No guys here but me and you, Craig."

I take a step forward, closing the gap between us. I've got the gas nozzle pointed at Beau's barrel chest. "You, Milligan, Briggs. I saw you on the phone. You rounding up the old crew? Trying to get the jump on me?"

Beau looks stunned. I guess he underestimated my ability to see right through him. But he has no idea what I've got planned tonight.

"Look," he says. "I don't hang out with those guys anymore." His face turns solemn as a priest's. "Not since I got cleaned up."

A chuckle sputters out of me. "The grease monkey's gone clean?" And then I remember the rumors. Corey Briggs became a cokehead. Jake Milligan got hooked on meth. And Beau? Painkillers, I think.

His face reddens. His jaw stiffens. He looks half-embarrassed, half-furious. Which half is going to win? He shuts his eyes and sighs. "Listen, Craig. I came out here to apologize. To make amends for times when I—"

"No, no, no." I shake my head, and the motion makes my brain go swimmy. When was the last time I ate a solid meal? "Save me all that Twelve-Step shit, all right?" I clank the nozzle back into its slot on the fuel pump. "You're forgiven, or whatever." I wave him off and fall into my car.

Back on the road, all the adrenaline drains from my body. In its place, a murky weight descends.

I'M JUST MINUTES AWAY from Janey's house when my cell phone rings. Her smiling face glows bright on the screen, but I already know what she's going to say, and my mood drops deeper still. My wife would say I'm too "emotionally detached" to have premonitions, but what does she know? Sure enough, Janey has to cancel. The babysitter couldn't make it, no one else is available at such short notice, she was really looking forward to catching up, et cetera.

"No problem," I grumble, and hang up. Truth be told, I'm more hungry now than horny. But I can't imagine dealing with other people—not even the cashier at a Mickey D's drive-thru. From the glove compartment, I fish out my flask and a bag of stale peanuts. Turning down a side street, I head further out into the boonies. No streetlights. Just farmland, citrus groves, and the murky outlines of houses and barns. Just salty peanuts and whiskey's sweet burn. On an impulse, I pull onto a gravel road. Little bits of scenery here look familiar—that horse stable, that pomegranate tree—but this town has become a dream version of itself. I know every rut in this road, but I couldn't tell you its name. Something Lane, Whatever Way.

I round a wide curve, and I spot the turn I didn't even know I was looking for. There's no sign, but instinct tells me it's the right way to go. Between the shadowy blades of a giant yucca plant and a lemon tree's gnarled limbs, I edge my car down a narrow drive. Half a mile later, I come up alongside a stand of mature oaks. I remember them well. My best friend from grade school, Scottie Jessell, used to live down here. His grandfather founded the granite quarry at the end of this road. And, on the far side of those oaks, he built the Jessell family home. On Saturday afternoons, while our moms gossiped on the porch, Scottie and I would ride our bikes beneath the rangy canopy of trees, down to the abandoned quarry. Granite boulders spilled all across the valley below, and Scottie and I would play reckless games on the rocky mounds.

My headlights flash on the metal crossbeam at the quarry's edge. I stop in a thundercloud of dust.

The night air is mild. A half moon lights up one small circle of the world at a time. When I was a kid, I'd scramble over that crossbeam, sure-footed and quick. Thirty years later, it's an awkward climb followed by a stiff landing that jars my knees. But, as I descend into the valley, the ache fades away. It's like I'm walking back through time. Past sagebrush and patches of wild grass, I hike down to a wide plateau, where the boulders jut from the earth.

Scottie and I, we developed a system of dares: a sequence of jumps between the rocks, each gulf wider than the last. The map of that progression is etched into my brain. I step onto the starting rock, and there's nowhere else I'd rather be. The first jump is more like a hop—barely six inches of empty space between granite ledges. I could step across, but it's going airborne that matters. So I bend my knees and leap. Even with that short distance, I feel the old weightless freedom. The old thrill.

Scottie and I never admitted to our parents that we played in the quarry. Mom would have been horrified by such risky behavior. But what was her reward for a life of caution? Stomach cancer, and the looming specter of death. Dad, on the other hand, never cared what I did. I got into plenty of scrapes as a kid. A couple of times, I needed stitches. But that didn't stop me from playing hard. Just like a little danger never stopped Dad from smoking indoors. About once a year, he would set the couch ablaze, and we'd all go running for the fire extinguisher. A house fire—that's probably what'll kill the old man. Hey, better to burn up than fade away, right?

The second jump is easy. The third and fourth jumps, too. I make them all from a standing start. The next jump is maybe a yard across. In the pale light, the boulder on the far side of the divide is just a char-colored mass. When I close my eyes, the long years disappear, and I see its daylight form. I take one step back and spring over the void. I land with a grunt, and the soles of my shoes skid on a patch of scree. My ass hits the granite before I know I'm falling. A fiery shock rifles up my spine. After a minute, the pain mellows enough that I manage to push myself upright.

Now, maybe I haven't exactly *cheated* death, but the flirtation is enough to get my blood pumping hot again.

The sixth jump. With a running start, I throw myself across the chasm. The balls of my feet strike the far boulder's edge, and I wobble backwards. My arms windmill, like in a cartoon. Somehow, the crazy flapping works, and I remain planted on the rock. As a kid, that sixth jump was the farthest I ever made. Scottie, too. We were Tyler's age then. Around that same time, Scottie and I got into a fistfight over the ownership of some damn comic book. After that, we didn't talk for years. Not until a house party in high school, when Scottie got shit-faced and cornered me in a hallway. "I made the seventh jump, Craig." Eyes all woozy, he shook his finger at me. "More than you ever did. Wuss." I told Scottie I had no idea what he was talking about and pushed him aside. But of course I knew. I believed him, too.

I pace to the back of the boulder and turn. Inky shapes, that's all I see. How wide is the gap: Six feet? Nine? The exact measure doesn't matter. The seventh jump is the seventh jump. I take strong, steady breaths. I'm nodding my head. *Yeah, yeah, yeah.* My nerves are tingling—energy pulsing at my hip.

No, that's just my phone vibrating. And there's Janey's face again.

"Hey," she says. "The babysitter pulled through after all. Are you still free?"

For a moment, I'm tempted to invite her down to the quarry. The surface of the silvery rocks glow beneath the moon—like only magical things could happen in that spot. But I won't find magic between Janey Hopstetter's thighs. I've had affairs before. They all end the same: five seconds of ecstasy that withers into weeks of regret.

"Sorry," I say. "I already made other plans. Maybe next time I'm in town?"

After we hang up, it hits me—the next time I'm home, it'll probably be for Mom's funeral.

I take a swig from my flask, and the whiskey tumbles down with a good, rough bite. Why do I want the seventh jump more than I want Janey? It's not like I really care what Scottie thinks of me. Or Beau, or LeeAnn, or my shitty dad, or even my dying mom. Why, then? Something like fate, I suppose. Tonight, I've wandered onto the backroads of history. Before adulthood. Before marriage and kids and failing careers. Before ailing parents and receding hairlines and filings for divorce. Before we ached for anything in life but the bright and trembling now. Really, what else is there?

I shake out the stiffness that's settled into my limbs. My eyes focus on the dark and distant mass awaiting my arrival. Between one precipice and the next, a great plunge awaits— the drop into nowhere. I'm bouncing on my toes, ready for the leap. If I'm lucky? I won't ever land.

Clean Mojave Light

From our Los Angeles driveway east to Yucaipa, Mom's classical station filled our wood panel wagon with sweeping concertos and stately quartets. Somewhere in the flatlands of the Morongo Valley, the pleading strings of Barber's "Adagio" bled into static. Dad killed the radio. My sister Jeannie and I knew from experience not to request Top 40 or rock. "I can't drive with that crap on," Dad would say. And so, for the next hour, the Tully family moved in silence across the spare desert terrain.

We angled north onto a crackled two-lane highway—a slow ascent through the Transverse Ranges. Dad's steel attaché case slid out from under the front seat, bumping against the toes of my sneakers. He carried that case every time he conducted corporate business. Dad worked as a Data Analyst in a gray concrete building downtown and traveled frequently. He prepared summaries, he wrote prospectuses. I knew no other details of his job. Dad was like that attaché case: hard, inscrutable, and locked shut. I nudged the case back into its hiding place.

It was Mom's idea to turn Dad's business trip into our summer vacation. That night, he had a meeting scheduled with Erno Laukkanen, his Corporate Associate in Las Vegas. We all had reservations at Caesars Palace, where Centurions roamed a marble lobby and Roman columns bordered an

Olympic swimming pool made of real Italian marble. Mom got us tickets to see Cher at Circus Maximus, Jeannie had saved up her allowance for shopping, and Dad promised to take me to the new Omnimax Theatre, where they projected "The Eruption of Mount St. Helens!" onto the roof of a giant dome.

But first we had to get there. In the middle of a global energy crisis, fuel pumps ran dry all across Southern California. Dad refused again and again to endure the lines of cars that coiled around service stations like rattlesnakes. "No way, José," he said each time. "We'll have better luck at the next one."

Our engine died in sputters and gasps at the edge of a town called Desert Sands. Dad coasted the wagon down the offramp, his meaty neck throbbing. We rolled to a stop along the dusty shoulder of the road. A handful of businesses and a smattering of homes poked up from the sagebrush and scrabble, but no signs of life stirred.

"Oh, boy." Jeannie rolled her eyes. "What a super place you've discovered, Dad."

My sister had a flair for protest that I lacked. I stayed quiet, waiting for our parents to take charge.

Mom freed herself from the car and lit a Virginia Slim. "Shall I scout ahead then?" She taught Latin at a women's college and moved with finishing school poise. She strolled into town as if the scorched air buoyed her stride.

Dad leaned out the window. "Sure, abandon your family in its time of need. That's wonderful, Meg. Just fantastic."

Jeannie and I exchanged a look. Even she seemed wary of Dad's simmering rage. We unstuck ourselves from the back seat and tumbled out into the solemn heat. We spit into our palms, and our flesh sizzled against the metal of the rear bumper. Jeannie was a high school track star. She leveraged her powerful legs against the old station wagon, while I grunted and skidded on the loose grit. I'd just turned fourteen and had earned the nickname Stick Figure Billy. As Dad liked to joke: "When the kid turns sideways, he disappears."

Eventually, we gained momentum. Jeannie and I muscled the station wagon into the meager heart of Desert Sands. "NO GAS," read the cardboard sign taped to the lone fuel pump at the Arco station. We were doomed. No way would we make it to Vegas that day. No Centurions, no Cher, no shopping, no volcanos. And no Olympic pool. I stopped pushing altogether and let gravity take its course.

Jeannie glared at me over her shoulder. "Gosh, thanks!"

I scraped the sweat off my brow and shuffled along behind.

A moving van passed by, coughing into a higher gear as it thundered out of town. Through the gray fog of its exhaust, I spotted Mom across the road. She entered the front office of the Motel California, its neon sign pulsing in teal and pink.

Jeannie gave the wagon a final push, and Dad pulled hard on the powerless steering wheel. Our car settled into the empty gravel parking lot outside the motel, where a neat row of a dozen doors lined the white stucco wall. Above the motel's flat roof, the bright blue sky and the ragged peaks of the San Bernardinos loomed.

Seconds later, Mom emerged from the manager's office, dangling two room keys from her slender hand. "It's not exactly Caesar's Palace," she said. "But we've got the place to ourselves, according to Don back there."

We peered through the office window. Don waved his pudgy hand, a look of embarrassment—or possibly apology—in his eyes.

"Come on, Jeannie." Mom locked arms with my sister. "We girls will hole up in 101." She dangled a room key at Dad, but set her green speckled eyes on me. "Billy, you're stuck with your father in 102."

I BOUGHT A BOTTLE of orange soda from the vending machine near Don's office and filled our ice bucket. When I got back to the room, Dad flipped shut his steel attaché and pushed it under his bed.

From his thermos, Dad poured nut-brown liquor into one of the glasses from the bathroom vanity. With a pair of plastic tongs, he dropped three ice cubes into his drink. "Do you hear that buzz?" He kicked off his shoes and wandered the room. "A kind of humming, like?"

Dad had a habit of talking to himself. With his attention scattered among the fixtures and furnishings, I couldn't tell whether he expected a response from me.

He slanted his ear against the door that adjoined our room to the rest of the Tully clan. "Ha. The girls are watching some goddamned soap opera. Even through two inches of plywood, you can hear the inane dialogue."

That would be Jeannie. Didn't he know that Mom hated soaps? Besides, I'd just seen her out by the tiny swimming pool, sitting alone with a magazine.

Dad turned and walked in short, even paces down the center line of the room. "But that's no TV I'm hearing out here. Nuh-uh." He paused beneath the yellow dome of the overhead light fixture. With thick fingers, he unscrewed the nut that held the plastic covering in place. "Just like twisting the nipple on a nice, round tit." And there came his cobra smile—a twisty sneer that always made me cringe.

A lively knock danced against our door.

Dad held the yellow dome in his palm, inspecting its smooth surface. "Check who that is. If you see a big blonde idiot, let him in."

On the other side of the peephole stood a man in a wide-collared shirt and white bell-bottomed jeans. Solid and tall, his yellow hair fell in waves down to his jawline.

I opened the door, just as a pickup truck overloaded with furniture and suitcases banked onto the highway's northbound lane. Our family should have been headed that way, too.

"Ah, you must be Bill!" Erno Laukkanen flowed past me into the room, trailed by a citrusy scent.

I liked his shortening of my name. Bill. It had a solid resonance. I'd gone by Billy my entire life, and it had never occurred to me that I could simply lop off that infantilizing final syllable. I'd just graduated from junior high, which meant a new school in the fall. Could I become someone named Bill?

"Hello, Dave." Erno tilted his head and smirked at my father. "Okay, so how many Data Analysts does it take to change a lightbulb?"

"There's a noise in the room." Dad tapped the metal fitting around the naked bulb. "You know the noise I mean, Erno? Somewhere between a hum and a buzz?" Then he screwed the dome back into place.

"Well, Dave. If I ever meet an actual Data Analyst, I'll ask him. Ha, ha." Erno sniffed the mouth of Dad's thermos. "It's a good thing I packed a cooler. Vodka will prove necessary this evening, I think." He spun a smooth one-eighty and faced me.

I hadn't moved from the slim patch of wall between window and door.

Erno had clear Scandinavian eyes, the blues of a glacial bay. "Has your father told you much about me, Bill? No? Well, I grew up in a Lapland village in the far north of Finland, within pissing distance of the Russian border. But that was before the Iron Curtain. Before Major Dave Tully and I served together at a research base in the Arctic Sea. Before I married a girl from Baltimore and became a U.S. citizen."

"Hey, Lucinda was my girl first." Dad narrowed his eyes at Erno.

"Oh, Dave. You got over that pretty quickly, as I recall." Erno turned back to me. "Your father was best man at our wedding! But, so, yes. Before the wedding and before Lucinda filed for divorce . . . before all of that, Bill, I was born into the dark magic of the natural world. You see, I come from mixed parentage. My mother was a polar bear. And my father, he was a drunk!" Erno tossed back his golden head and laughed up at the ceiling.

I failed to grasp his jokes, but I laughed along anyway. The man had saved me from the stagnating atmosphere of that room.

Dad snatched up his drink and returned to pacing the floor.

SUNSET FELL HEAVY, spilling red and orange across the barren landscape that surrounded the Motel California. Around the flagstone patio, lights flickered awake. Mom sat in a chaise longue at the edge of the pool. She called out to Dad: "It's not exactly Olympic, is it? In terms of size, I mean." Around her swimsuit, Mom wore a floral sarong. She tapped the ashes of her cigarette into a potted palm and sipped a vodka martini prepared by Erno Laukkanen.

Jeannie sat next to Mom, rambling in her animated way—flourishes of manicured nails, dramatic eyerolls, and hiccupping laughs. She'd been gabbing for hours about boys she liked, friends she didn't like, the grossness of her driver's ed instructor, the relative merits of clothing brands, every show on television, dance routines. A monologue of girl stuff that I barely registered. Mom's end of the conversation was monosyllabic: "Mm-hm," and "Yeah," and "Gee." Meanwhile, Mom's gaze wandered the darkening foothills, lost in whatever daydreams the saguaros cradled in their arms.

Between bursts of speech, my sister massaged the tuning dial of the silver transistor radio that rested in her lap. She skipped back and forth between pop stations—one from Los Angeles and the other from Las Vegas. But Desert Sands lay in the staticky crux of two pulsating worlds.

Dad stood inside the gloaming of Erno's doorway, his thermos in one hand and that glass from the bathroom sink in the other. He stared at the light fixture above the glass door, shaking his head.

Despite the radio's poor reception, Erno grooved to the music. He'd placed his enormous cooler on a patio table outside room 103. While mixing cocktails, he sang along with Blondie and shook his hips to Village People. He tipped vodka into plastic tumblers, then danced the drinks across the patio to "the ladies"—a martini for Mom and a virgin daiquiri for Jeannie.

Nursing another orange soda, I sat in a shaded chair. My swimming trunks were as dry as the blistered air. Mom wasn't the only one disappointed by the Motel California pool.

The scene reminded me of every other Tully family vacation I could remember, stranded or otherwise: Mom and Dad keeping to opposite sides of whatever space we occupied, Jeannie blabbing away at Mom, and me the outskirts. Would Vegas have been any different?

With no other distractions at hand, I flipped through the pages of my comic book, scanning the garish panels. Mutants battled their own identities, while shadowy realms of government tried to hunt them down. Were there mutants who possessed no special powers? Wouldn't some mutations make us weaker? I tried to reckon my own gawky frame against my father's compact force and my mother's lean grace. I was clearly the product of genetic devolution. Professor X would send me packing.

Between serving rounds of drinks, Erno spoke in low tones with my father. Corporate business, I supposed. The weak strains of Donna Summer's "Bad Girls" absorbed their words.

A few pages into my comic, I looked up to find Erno bustling toward the chaise longues with a fresh round of drinks. Gliding across the flagstones, his fingertips dipped into the cups of red and green and blue. "Why is Dave so sour, Meg? This weekend couldn't have turned out better."

Mom snorted. "Gee, really?" She took her fresh martini from Erno's hand and sucked a green olive from the end of a toothpick. "Because I'd pictured myself at Caesars right about now, eating a juicy cut of veal parmigiana at the Palace Court."

"Yeah, Meg?" Dad tipped back his watery scotch. "Well, I'm as close to Caesar as you're gonna get tonight. But I think I spotted a Golden Arches a few blocks down the road. Put a little extra ketchup on your cheeseburger, and you've got yourself a fine substitute for veal parmigiana."

"Har-dee-har." Mom raised her cup high. "Funny stuff, Dave."

"I come to bury Caesar," Erno said in stuffy baritone. "No, to praise him!" He turned an easy arc and slipped a drink into Jeannie's hand. "Another virgin daiquiri for the young lady." Erno flashed a wink at my sister, then pointed my way. "One for you, Bill? Or another orange soda?"

Stunned that he remembered me, I mutely shook my head. That very morning, Dad had driven halfway down the block before he realized I wasn't in the car.

THE WORLD BEYOND the Motel California soon slipped into darkness. The swimming pool glowed—an eerie hypnosis of underwater lighting, chlorine, and wavering heat. The flame of a Bic lighter sparked from the chaise longues. Mom held a hand-rolled cigarette, pinched between finger and thumb. The flame met one end of the cigarette, and her lips met the other. She sucked in that first drag of smoke, and a soft rapture lifted into her eyes. I understood then what burned inside. "Mm-hm," she said, and passed the joint to Jeannie. My sister inhaled deep and long.

If such a moment had previously occurred in the Tully family history, I hadn't witnessed it. I glanced over at Dad, but his eyes were focused on some remote spot in the night.

The poolside lights carried gray swirls of smoke across the patio. I sniffed at the musk that came my way, and just those few stray molecules swayed my brain. I craved more, but the world of drugs was alien to me. Smoking pot belonged to the older kids—the ones who partied and cut class and made out with their girlfriends. Sure, there were times when I wanted nothing more than to slip free of this troubled plane. But I also longed for the opposite: to become, to be seen.

"Dancing Queen" streamed from the transistor. In the transparency of night, the sound turned bold and clear. Erno took the joint from Jeannie and drifted into a series of deft disco moves. He closed his eyes and smiled. "Ah, the true music of Scandinavia. Fuck all the old folk tunes. Fuck Sibelius and Grieg. ABBA is the good shit. Ladies, dance with me!"

"I don't know," Jeannie said. "I'm feeling kinda woozy. It's like there's this humming in my head?"

"Ha! I told you so." Dad slapped the doorframe. "Thank you, sweetheart, for substantiating my claim." Then he glowered at me.

Had my silence on the matter implied disbelief? I simply didn't have any wisdom to contribute. But Dad always suspected me of keeping secrets. Me, and everyone else.

Erno held a hand out to Mom. "Meg, it's up to you."

"Oh, okay." She lifted to her feet. "It's not exactly a Las Vegas nightclub, but I suppose I'll make do with a substitute." Mom began to sway and step, and Erno mirrored her motions. "Wasn't that your suggestion, Dave? To accept a substitute for what I truly wanted?'

Dad's face puckered. "Something like that."

Erno and Mom fell into a natural rhythm of bodily shifts and slides. He held her eyes, and, for the first time that day, Mom truly smiled. Beat by beat, the dancers grew more fluid. The song's chorus swelled and grooved, and the distance between limbs and hips collapsed. Mom's palm pressed against Erno's chest. His hand moved along her bare back. The nimble fingertips of Erno Laukkanen glided down the silk hibiscus and plumeria at bloom on Mom's sarong. Down and over and around, until his hand firmly cupped her bottom.

A rush of dread spilled through me, and I crumpled the comic book's pages in my nervy paws.

Dad pounced from the doorway. In the span of one "tambourine," he bolted across the patio and tore Erno from Mom's arms, sending her stumbling away.

Dad twisted Erno's arm behind his back. "Et tu, Brute?" He cantilevered Erno off the flagstone, the Finn's white loafers scissor-kicking in the air. "I've had enough of your disco Don Juan bullshit."

Erno tumbled loose, landing light as a cat burglar. "Dave!" Erno raised his hands and laughed. "Hey, come on now."

Dad tucked his chin and raised his fists, tight but loose: the stance of a prizefighter. He bounced on the toes of his scuffed brown shoes.

"No, god damn it!" Mom stomped her bare foot—a noiseless and futile referee.

More than ever, I understood that I had no power to affect whatever events were set to unfold. I could only watch.

Poised and coiled, Erno and Dad focused their attentions on one other's feints and weaves. One man would grin, while the other sneered. Then they traded expressions, neither of them willing to commit to the mood of the moment. Between them lay a history I barely knew. At fourteen, I couldn't imagine the complications that might arise from decades of grudges and admirations. All I understood of adult tensions was that they tended to build.

Dad landed a jab—an almost playful punch to Erno's sternum. He smirked, self-satisfied—the cobra smile.

Erno grunted, and the mischief in his eyes turned dark.

Jeannie sat up and scooted to the edge of her chaise longue, eyes wide. Did she root for Dad? Or Erno?

I wasn't sure how I felt, myself. But I wanted to see our father's mettle tested. I pictured the marks of combat on his face—a split lip or the dark iridescence of a swollen eye. And maybe I liked that picture in my mind.

Dad wheeled his arm at his opponent's face, and badly missed. Erno lunged forward, low and grappling. He sunk a shoulder into Dad's gut and grabbed at his shirt. They tumbled into a patio table. Chairs toppled, and metal shrieked against stone.

In that clattering spectacle, none of us heard Mom drag the potted palm to the lip of the swimming pool. None of us watched her peel off her sarong, or twirl the silk into a length of vibrant rope. And none of us witnessed the tethering of wrist to sarong, and sarong to potted palm.

The sound of the splash hit me, followed by the spray. I fumbled my comic book into the spindrift air.

The potted palm began its descent. The sarong rope pulled taut, and Mom lifted from the earth. Anybody else would have made that plunge look ugly, but my mother cut a neat arc into the pool, as if she might be judged on technique.

We stood transfixed by the strange beauty of her dive. We became the audience for a daring magic trick. Then the bedrock seemed to tilt. I ran—we all ran—to the edge of the pool. A funnel of water followed Mom down, and ripples echoed in perfect circles across the surface. Hovering in the depths, she appeared weightless, like an astronaut suspended in the immortal void. Her cheeks bulged with the air she'd taken from the world above, and her eyes zeroed in on Dad's face. The intensity of her stare beamed with a familiar scorn.

Everyone in my family knew that expression. One of its members had committed a wrong.

"Oh my god!" Jeannie's bare feet padded behind me, and a door banged shut.

Erno shucked off one white loafer and stooped for the other.

Dad's hand clapped around Erno's arm. "No way, pal. She doesn't need our help." He shouted down into the pool: "That woman is like a goddamn porpoise!" Then Dad's arm swung against my chest. "You neither, sport."

I stopped, shocked to find myself teetering on the edge of the pool. I'd followed a primal urge to save my mother—the one person in the world who acknowledged my existence. But I wouldn't have known how to rescue her, even if Dad had let me try.

"Dave, for Christ's sake." Erno shoved my father hard, launching him backwards. Erno kicked away his other shoe, pulled up a pant leg, and peeled a Bowie knife from its leather sheath. With the dull edge of the blade clamped between his teeth, he executed a swashbuckler's dive into the swimming pool.

Even as I stood in rigid panic, I felt awed by the cinematic splendor. All of life was a movie that happened to me, the action directed by others.

Chaotic swirls of refracted light and motion overtook the pool. Potting soil spread like a cloud. I fell to my hands and knees, trying to decipher the sloshing dimensions.

My mother then burst to the surface. She sputtered and blinked, born again into life above water.

Erno followed, vaulting himself out of the pool. He took hold of Mom's slender wrists and hoisted her onto the patio, where she folded down to the flagstones and collapsed.

I expected Erno to fall upon my mother—to administer the chest-thumpings and wide-mouthed kisses of resuscitation. But Erno only patted her back. "So, you are okay then?"

Mom coughed. "Yes." Head lowered, she appeared transfixed by the slow spread of water that ran off her body. "Yes. Thank you." Her voice came nasal and tremulous, like a child shamed to the brink of tears.

"Now see what you did, Meg?" Dad lay where he'd landed, splayed on the patio. He looked strangely content, like an emperor lazing on a stone dais. "You ruined one of Erno's lady-killer shirts."

With a frown, Erno wrung out the puckering fabric that clung to his chest.

The door to the manager's office thumped open, and Jeannie ran toward us. "Mom, Mom, Mom!" She kneeled at our mother's side, massaging her arms with urgent strokes.

Donald trotted behind, clutching a first aid kit and a pair of scissors. On seeing Mom freed from the bottom of his shrunken swimming pool, he skidded to a halt. "Oh, whew! What a scare. Hoo-boy!"

Dad pulled himself into a patio chair. "I'm just dandy, by the way. Thanks for your concern, kids." I recognized that clamped jaw of his, that bitter squint. One fight had ended, and now the picking of a new fight began. "Enjoying all the sympathy, Meg? You oughta throw yourself into swimming pools more often."

I kept still, counting on my physique to disguise me as a lamppost, or as one of the potted palms not yet drowned by my family. During these parental skirmishes, I tried to flatten myself into a new dimension—one free of rancor and blame. It never worked.

Jeannie pushed her fingers through our mother's sopping hair. "Mom, what'd you do that for?"

Our mother cleared her throat. Between the bodies that crowded her, she fixed a sightline on Dad. "Alea iacta est."

Living in the household of a Latin teacher, my whole family knew its literal translation: "The die is cast." Julius Caesar spoke that famous phrase when crossing the river

Rubicon. A threshold breached. War declared. The point of no return.

MOM SHOOK ME AWAKE, and my first thought was that I'd missed the school bus. Then I saw the beige drapes, the ice bucket on the bureau, the matching twin beds. The Motel California. The front door stood ajar, and a wedge of sunlight fell across Dad's empty bed. From the bathroom came the white-noise roar of shower water.

"Come on, Billy. Get dressed quickly, okay?"

I smeared my palms across my eyes and pulled on yesterday's shorts and tee-shirt. I tugged on my sneakers, while Mom waited by the door. She held my suitcase in one hand and Dad's steel attaché in the other.

With a shudder of the pipes in the wall, the shower fell silent.

"Billy, let's go." Mom walked out the motel room door.

I grabbed my backpack and followed her outside, into the desert morning's glare.

Jeannie sat behind the wheel of the station wagon, a pair of dark sunglasses perched on her nose. Mom was tossing bags into the popped-open trunk. A red metal gas can sat next to the car.

Until that moment, I'd been following Mom's orders, still half asleep. Now my energies split, and I froze before the radiator grill. We were leaving? Without Dad? My lungs clamped tight around my heart.

Dad stomped out into the parking lot wearing nothing but a thin white towel around his waist. "What the hell's going on here?" The early light landed hard against his thick, pale flesh. Rivulets of water trickled through the hair on his legs and dripped off his toes. He stood beside me, breathing hard. "Jesus, Meg. You're making a getaway while I'm in the goddamn shower?"

Mom flung open the passenger door—a shield between her and my father. "A getaway? From you? No, you're always there, Dave—lurking around some corner. Except for when you flat-out disappear."

Mom and Dad continued like this: a volley of shouts and recriminations. I'd heard this fight before, too many times. But the turmoil never failed to claw at my chest. Breathless, I stood paralyzed in that no man's land.

Jeannie stared dead ahead, her face gone slack. She looked bored, but that was a trick she played on herself—a means of disassociation.

But I didn't share her talent. My trick was to hide. The safe haven of the backseat beckoned me forward. But Dad—glistening with fury—had placed himself between me and the wagon.

Beyond the Motel California parking lot, a suburban crammed with belongings rolled toward the highway, a VW Bug hitched to its towbar. The family inside looked relieved to be making their escape from that town.

Dad squinted, and the locus of his rage shifted away from Mom. "Okay, Jeannie." He jutted his chin back toward the motel. "Apparently, your mom can do whatever the hell she wants. But the rest of the Tully clan stays here. This is a family vacation, remember? Now get out of the damn car."

My sister turned to Mom. Between their gazes, some sort of telepathic conversation occurred. When Jeannie looked at Dad again, she simply shook her head.

"Aw, Christ." Dad threw up his arms.

I think we all expected the towel to fall, but it remained miraculously in place.

The door to room 103 swung open then, and Erno Laukkanen strolled into the parking lot. "The ladies are going for a drive?" His blonde hair fell flat and red lines crackled the blue of his eyes. He wore a faded tee-shirt with his white pants, now wrinkled and stiff. He shut his eyes against the sun, and it looked for a moment like sleep might reclaim him. Then Erno strode past me and fell into a single push-up on the motel room carpet. Empty-handed, he bounced upright and strode to the back of the station wagon. Seconds later, the trunk popped open.

"Hey!" Mom craned her head out the window. "What the hell?"

Erno shut the trunk and smiled—a ragged strain of yesterday's easy beam. "My apologies, Meg." He carried Dad's steel attaché case. "But this item was mistakenly packed with the other luggage."

"Meg, you dumb bitch." Dad cocked a fist and stretched one bare foot toward the open passenger window.

Erno blocked his momentum, just as Dad had blocked mine the night before.

There Mom sat, statue-like in her resolve. But a strain showed in the sharpness of her clavicles, in the furrows at her temples. She held our family's center, and a system of bodies gravitated around her. Those bodies sometimes lost their orbits and came hurtling toward her. I supposed she could only brace herself for impact. Or remove herself from the troubled system.

"Come on, Dave." Erno clamped a hand around Dad's shoulder. "You'll feel better with some pants on."

"The hell I will," Dad said. But he allowed Erno to lead him away from the car.

I felt the weight of their approach. If I stayed, I would be trapped with these men—and for who knows how long. I couldn't fathom the lonely hours of re-reading the same stupid comic books, sucking down orange sodas, and waiting for the arrival of gasoline to that dying town. So I made my move—a dash to the back door of the car. I pulled on the chrome handle and flung myself inside.

"God, Billy," Jeannie said. "You're such a spaz."

Dad sneered at me. "You, too? My whole family's deserting me now? Wonderful. You bunch of traitors."

Erno laughed. "Interesting choice of words there, Dave."

"Shut up, Erno."

Dad then pointed at Mom. "We're going to have a serious talk when I get home."

Mom cupped her hand to the side of her mouth. "You and my lawyer, Dave."

A curl came to Dad's lip, but not the full cobra. He looked defeated, in a way I'd never seen before. I almost felt sorry for leaving my father's side. But my elation in that moment overpowered any lingering sympathies I might have held.

Jeannie swanned her head around and threw the wagon in reverse. The car's tires growled over loose gravel. Just ahead lay the old two-lane highway. The road away from that miserable place. The road back home.

Erno Laukkanen held the attaché in one hand and waved with the other. Such a casual farewell, like we might see him again one day.

Dad just stood there. He grew smaller, fainter. His expression, indistinct as a stranger's. The stucco walls of the Motel California absorbed his white towel, his pale flesh. Brightness ricocheted off asphalt and windowpanes. That moment lasted for miles, for years. The world we left behind, erased by clean Mojave light.

The Lioness

Last night, Chloe dreamed of Ujasiri—the escaped Katanga lioness from the Oregon Zoo. In Chloe's dream, they'd encountered one another on a dusty savanna sprung forth from the concrete city. Young woman and stray beast had shared a telepathic exchange—wisdom that might guide Chloe through the labyrinth of her displacement. If only she could remember the wise words of that dream.

A stubborn drizzle coated the windows of her Aunt Isidore's ramshackle Victorian in Southeast Portland. Chloe sat at the lusterless kitchen table, hunched over her laptop and searching for news of Ujasiri. She coughed into the crook of her elbow—rumbling hacks muffled by a thick wool sweater. She felt trapped in the slipstream of time—caught between late night and early morning, between late winter and early spring, between old life and new. She had set herself drift in the marine zone—quiet, cold, and wet. She pressed her mug of hot black coffee to her cheeks.

The previous autumn, Chloe had fled Los Angeles, the land of her birth. Since her arrival in the Pacific Northwest, the muddle of days had collapsed into dense splotches in her lungs. *How could I have abandoned the sun?* Now she'd contracted a cold, or worse. *How could I leave my gig at the ad agency?* Last week, she'd started her third menial job in six months—cashier at a cupcake shop. *How could I …?*

No, she'd been right to dump her fiancée—that gorgeous liar. She'd discovered his affair with that vapid actress from the tampon commercial, the girl with the broad smile and carefree white apparel. The betrayal had metastasized inside Chloe, leaving dark stains in every corner of her life. She'd considered retreating to the sanctuary of her childhood bedroom, with meals prepared by Mom. But she needed change, she yearned to grow. So, Chloe scissored herself from the map of California and drove to the City of Roses, where life bloomed anew.

Now she paid three hundred dollars a month to live in her cranky aunt's sewing room. Izzy the herbalist, Izzy the spinster. Izzy the family weirdo.

Chloe pushed a damp shank of hair across her forehead. She sipped her coffee and browsed local news sites for updates on Ujasiri's whereabouts. The animal's means of escape continued to baffle the zookeepers. At the start, they'd suspected abduction. Then a hiker came across the great cat's prints in the soft, wet earth of Forest Park. The following night, a homeless teenager claimed to have seen a lion near the railroad tracks that fed into Union Station. The next day, a woman discovered the eviscerated body of her pet goat. It hung limp from a nearby oak, like a coat draped on a hook.

Chloe had visited the Zoo the previous month, on a rare sunbreak day. In the heart of the lion enclosure, Ujasiri had stood on the lip of a large gray boulder, certain and strong. The lioness, with her sharp bronze eyes, had stripped Chloe bare of all her self-deceptions. She'd found herself reduced to a single thought: *How did I screw up my life so badly?* Held there in the gaze of Ujasiri, a calm new voice had sounded in her mind: *Girl, you chose well to escape the cage of your old life. Why do you now turn your new home into yet another cage?* On that afternoon, Chloe took the lioness for her spirit guide. Ujasiri, a Swahili word, meant courage. An elusive quality,

Chloe's own courage had disappeared somewhere near the Oregon state line.

Across the coffee's steaming surface, she breathed a thin stream of air, and a new volley of coughs heaved from her chest. From the second floor, old wooden planks creaked. Aunt Izzy: awoken.

In Chloe's remaining moments of solitude, she clicked and scrolled through one final newsfeed. All the media outlets ran the same video clip of Ujasiri—the golden lioness at prowl, stalking the confines of her pen, amber eyes burning bright. But the website offered no new updates. Nothing since yesterday's gored goat.

A thicket of gray-brown hair appeared in the doorframe. Izzy shuffled into the kitchen, bundled in her faded purple bathrobe, deep frown-lines scraped into her face. Below the rough surface, the gentle features of Chloe's mother—Izzy's younger sister—shone through. Eyes that might turn soft like Mom's, arms that might embrace.

"Aw, damn. Sorry I woke you up, Iz."

Her aunt sighed. She lit the burner underneath the tarnished silver kettle, then leaned over Chloe's laptop. "Stick out your tongue."

"Why do you want—?"

The wrinkles around Izzy's eyes tightened. "Tongue."

Chloe threw back her head, dropped her jaw, and thrust out her tongue. She knew she was being petulant, and a new level of shame seeped into her heart. She felt reduced, distanced from the womanhood she'd begun to forge for herself back in Los Angeles. Her spirit spun in retrograde.

Izzy grumbled, then swung open the pantry—her cabinet of mysterious remedies. She retrieved mason jars crammed with dry, brown vegetative things. Her fingers pinched and plucked, depositing the ingredients into a metal tea infuser. Soon, the kitchen smelled like the moldering of a felled tree. Then the kettle whistled—an urgent and lonely sound. Her aunt poured steaming water into the sad ochre mug that Chloe always pushed to the back of the cupboard. From its brim, the infuser's thin silver chain hung like the tail of a drowned rat.

"Hey, Iz, did you hear about that escaped lion?"

"Hmph." Izzy plunked down the steeping tea in front of Chloe. "That cat had it good back in the zoo, where she belonged. And now she's gotten herself into a real mess."

Chloe frowned into the brown liquid. "Yeah, I guess."

"Now, drink up. My tea'll heal you faster than any of that Western medicine crap." And then her aunt was gone—the warped wooden stairs complaining as Izzy retreated back to bed.

Chloe stirred the tea. A sharp and bitter vapor wisped inside her. She sipped from the chipped mug and felt her face pucker tight. The brew tasted of land, of moss, of bark. It left a tingle, or maybe a sizzle, on her tongue. In three hard swallows, she gulped it down. But the bitterness lingered in her mouth, and the mucous continued to flow. If she appeared at the bakery oozing snot, they would send her home. And, if the illness lingered, her boss might let her go entirely. Send her packing, give her the heave ho. But Chloe needed that job—for the money, for her pride. *I'm gonna sell some cupcakes today, goddamn it.* Chloe rummaged a bottle of NyQuil from her backpack. With a quick chug of green syrup, she chased away the tea's boggy residue. Her whole body shuddered, like the aftershock of gulping tequila.

Chloe made her way to the mudroom. The brief trek brought a muzzy warmth to her head. Her chest burned, and she leaned against a doorjamb until her breathing eased. In her aunt's filigreed antique mirror, webs of red lines crackled across Chloe's eyes. Eyes so wide and bright last summer, now turned weary and dull.

She tugged on her pink rain jacket, its neon floral print chosen as a cheerful talisman against the gray pallor of

Portland in wintertime. But the jacket failed to bolster her mood. Her beloved car—a vintage baby blue Volkswagen Beetle—sat idle in Izzy's garage, its engine dead. So, Chloe wrangled her bicycle out the back door, her headlamp illuminating the infinitude of raindrops that fell through the pre-dawn sky. Only three blocks to the city bus that would carry her downtown, then another eight blocks to the bakery. That much, she could do.

Chloe pedaled down the empty street, the bike wobbling beneath the unsteady pumping of her legs. From a hundred feet away, she heard the hydraulic cough and groan of the bus as it pulled away from her stop and revved down the street. At that time of the morning, the next bus wouldn't come for half an hour. If she waited, she'd be late. Chloe blinked away the swell of stupid, useless tears. Crying was for California. Chloe snorted hard and spat a thick glob of phlegm onto the gleaming asphalt. Then she pedaled on.

Under dripping trees, she rode past darkened homes. Brave rose bushes bloomed, despite late winter's miserly chill. The city blocks melted away, and she glided riverward. Inside the wells of her skull, dammed-up cavities loosened. A vaporous rush filled her head, and a fragment of Ujasiri's dream message shook free. *I descend from those who roam the Namib Desert, from those who journey to the banks of Lake Upemba to lap its cool blue waters. That great domain is my birthright. Instead, my mother bore me inside the confines of a cage. But now this city of forest and rain is my home. I will adapt to its patterns and laws. I will thrive.*

Thrive. As Chloe swept across the Hawthorne Bridge, she felt so far away from that state of power and grace.

Downtown Portland lay before her, with its ghost of a skyline—yellow windows that hovered against the dark curves of the West Hills. Her body warmed itself against the cold air, and a good sweat gathered along her forearms and scalp. Or maybe a bad sweat. She felt light, and also lightheaded. Cars rattled by, their headlights dancing off the bridge's latticed girders. Glare, glare, glare. Chloe angled away her gaze, toward the Willamette River below. From beneath the bridge, the prow of a Dragon Boat emerged, oars slicing through the blue-black waters. And did the dragon release that roar? No, that must've been the shout of the coxswain.

Down the offramp, Chloe coasted into Waterfront Park. Through the green pitch of dewy grass, she weaved onto the esplanade. The cold rain clung to her face, and her head swooned. A rush of blood, a tilted whirl. She squinted, gripping the handlebars tight, and swung below the western span of the Morrison Bridge. There, in the darkest shadows of the concrete buttresses, her headlamp caught a shank of tawny fur. She broke into a hard skid. Her lungs clamped tight against the frantic hammering of her heart. *Turn around and pedal away. No, make no sudden movements!* Chloe held still, locked in an awkward stance astride her bike.

Ujasiri stood before her. The lioness glared, fierce in the glow. She swished her tail along the ground in a mighty sweep, crisp as the whisking of a broom. And Chloe saw that her hide wasn't so much golden as yellow-brown—like dead grass and parched land. From Ujasiri's throat, a low and rattling growl reverberated.

Chloe willed herself to breathe—the only action she could muster. She measured the distance between bodies: two bounds and one fatal leap. Near enough that the scent of the animal—a musk of dirt, blood, pheromone, and dampened hide—caught in Chloe's throat. She swayed.

But Ujasiri didn't pounce. Instead she bent her head to a lumpen thing wedged between her massive paws. An animal of some kind, belly up and splayed. Ujasiri crunched her jaws into the belly of her prey.

From the embankment behind Chloe, someone shouted. "Oh, no, no!"

Chloe risked a glance over her shoulder.

A hooded man skidded down the slick grass slope. He was bearded and bundled in coats.

Chloe shook her head and raised her hand at the man's approach. This crazed stranger would rile Ujasiri. He'd get them killed.

"Oh, no, no, no, no, no." He stopped at Chloe's side. His odor of old cigarettes and sweated-out booze commingled with the musk and offal that Ujasiri stirred into the air.

Chloe breathed through her mouth, trying not to retch.

"That's my dog." The homeless man pulled his arms into an X, tight across his chest. His body rocked, heel-to-toe, urgent as a firehouse bell. A system of vibrations, his voice shook, too. "Fucking lion got my Daisy. Oh man, oh man. Oh, Daisy, Daisy, Daisy."

Ujasiri ignored her human observers. She settled down on the concrete, in the dry patch beneath the underpass. She was probably accustomed to people gawking while she ate. Ujasiri dipped her snout into her quarry, and blood dripped from her muzzle.

Chloe unclenched her fingers from the bicycle's hand brakes. In slow and careful steps, she scooted backward, away from the lioness. Away from death.

But the homeless man remained, rocking and transfixed.

Chloe tugged the sleeve of his sweatshirt. "Come on," she whispered. "Your dog …?" She tugged harder. "Sorry, but you gotta come on."

The vibrating man grew still, then shuffled in backpedal alongside Chloe. They retreated up the path until they'd reached the street above. All the way, he muttered his chant: "Daisy, Daisy, Daisy, Daisy."

What else did he have in this world? Nothing, as far as Chloe could see. She pulled her wallet from her backpack. She had eleven dollars. If she didn't get fired, she could take an advance against her paycheck. "Here," she said, and held the bills out to the homeless man.

His gaze stayed locked on the underpass. The soft light of the new day lit the esplanade, but the lioness and her carnage remained in shadow. He took the money. "Won't buy me a new dog."

Chloe shook her head, but he wouldn't have noticed. She hoped he'd spend the money on cheap booze. Get loaded and drink a toast to Daisy. Do whatever it took to survive the day.

And that's all that mattered to Ujasiri, too. Survival. Chloe's dream of the wise, ennobled beast? Total bullshit.

She mounted her bicycle seat. The rain had stopped, and the eastern sky lightened, from deep indigo to lavender, like the healing of a bruise. Chloe pushed her feet against the pedals, feeling stronger as the city blocks blurred with speed. She might still make it to the bakery on time. She could call animal control, or whoever, while counting out the till. Then she'd light up the display cases and open shop. Chloe would gladly sate all comers—anyone whose entrance caused the door to chime. Did such a day count as thriving? Or just surviving? She no longer cared. She was alive. Alive, and ready to sell some goddamn cupcakes.

Beyond the Gatehouse

Zane swerved his old Jeep down the rutted dirt road. He loved a good bumpy ride. But maybe Paul didn't share his enthusiasm. The kid bounced around in the passenger seat, his scrawny limbs flailing as he grappled for handholds. In his canary yellow sweatshirt, he looked like a Sesame Street reject. Paul belonged to Zane's girlfriend, Saundra, and they all lived together in an old farmhouse on the outskirts of Bumfuck, Washington. Did that mean the kid belonged to Zane now, too?

"Hang on there, man!" Zane gave Paul a grin and a wink. They were having fun, right? Boys on a backwoods ramble. Strong winter fog. Pines, ferns, and blackberry brambles. Just the kind of rugged excursion Zane would've loved when he was fourteen. But his dad was a bus driver. Once he got off work, he refused to get behind the wheel of a car. The old man spent his nights sitting on the living room sofa with a can of Schlitz, cursing at the Indians or the Browns.

Paul looked a little seasick, with that miserable stare and his face gone extra pale. The kid had one of those delicate constitutions that Zane had never understood. Too much of a mama's boy, maybe? Saundra and Paul's dad divorced ages ago, and he now lived with an actress in Malibu. So, the kid lacked what you'd call a reliable father figure. But the idea of becoming some kind of stepfather scared the shit out of Zane. He just wanted to stay on Saundra's good side by spending some quality time with her only child.

Zane had told Paul they were heading out on an adventure. Looked at another way, it was a drug run into the middle of nowhere. Zane's dealer was a guy named Fresno, an ex-hippie gun nut hiding out in the forest—in a place he called the Gatehouse. The house itself was just a regular one-story ranch. But he always had these cute chicks shacked up with him. And, out back, old Indian ruins poked up between the moss and trees. Good shit for a teenage boy, right?

Anyway, the kid needed to get out and see the world. Paul had spent his entire holiday break drawing comic books on his computer, with crappy pop music blaring through his headphones. Hooked up to all those machines, he looked like a cancer patient on life support.

The Jeep teetered around a hard curve, splashing brown puddle water through the air. Paul winced up at Zane from the passenger seat.

Zane shrugged. He drummed on the steering wheel, his speakers crackling with the nasty guitar lick that kicked off "Life in the Fast Lane." For years, that song was Zane's mantra. He'd lived for the slip-slide thrill. And every second had felt so damn full. But now, closing in on forty, the empty days started to stack up. Zane woke up feeling ragged, with aches that dragged across the hours. When night came, he and Saundra snorted coke and screwed 'til dawn. No need for sleep because neither of them had steady jobs. Saundra had inherited the house from her grandparents, so they had no mortgage to pay. On occasion, Zane hung some drywall. And Saundra found temp work here and there. Mostly, they lived off the alimony checks from Paul's dad. He made a killing cooking the books for Hollywood movie studios—what did he care where the money went?

"So, this Gatehouse place?" Paul shouted over Joe Walsh's guitar solo. "It's around here somewhere?"

"Yeah." Zane squinted into the blur of evergreen and fog. Late afternoon, and almost no light filtered through. "There's a tricky left coming up. Kind of easy to miss." And maybe he'd already missed the turn—a narrow gap in the woods that, on previous runs, had opened wide at his approach. He drove on, cursing himself for not replacing those damn headlights. The right bulb burned out two years ago. Then, last week, he'd smashed the left headlight into a tree.

Zane stabbed out his cigarette in the ashtray and slipped a toothpick from his pocket. He bit down on the wood. Thanks to that little habit, he'd cut back from two packs of Camels a day to just the one.

The road narrowed further still.

Paul braced both hands against the metal dash. "You sure we're going the right way?"

The road was no longer a road. Life in the non-lane. Zane stomped on the brakes, just to give the kid a little jolt. "No, Paul. I'm not so fucking sure, all right?"

"Okay. Jesus." Paul crossed his arms and scrunched his chin into a pout.

"You think you know shit? You do, I can tell. Well, man, I remember being fourteen. A cocksure punk. So, let me tell you something, Paul. Your eyes are only just starting to open up."

Paul shrugged. "Whatever."

"You look at me like I'm just a storm blowing through. But I'm in this for the long haul, kid. Here I am. Here I fucking am." Zane sighed. He'd meant to sound triumphant, but he'd tired out mid-speech. Too little sleep, nothing to eat this morning but beef jerky and half a cup of yesterday's coffee. Now his skull felt both swollen and shrunk tight. "All right. I've said my piece." He spit out his toothpick, lit a fresh cigarette, and cranked the gearshift into reverse.

That dead-end spot held the Jeep in a bearhug. Turning around would require some maneuvering, and the patience

Zane tended to lack. He wiped a smudge from the dashboard clock. Night fell early that time of year. A quick drop from winter gray to black.

ZANE DRAGGED his stiff muscles out of the Jeep. Once he'd finally jockeyed his way out of that bottleneck back in the woods, the hidden turnoff to the Gatehouse had showed itself right away—like a neon sign flickering to life. Open for business.

Paul stayed in the passenger seat. Arms and legs locked in place, he wanted Zane to know he remained pissed off. And the Gatehouse, with its chipped paint and weedy yard, wouldn't lure anybody toward its door. Knowing Fresno, he'd probably planned it that way.

"No heat in that Jeep without these." Zane dangled his keyring and headed down the gravel path to the front door. "And the cute girls are thisaway." He knocked on the door. He jammed his fists into the pockets of his sheepskin coat and bounced on his toes. Zane's breath streamed white into the late afternoon air.

Paul appeared at his side, slouchy with disappointment. Or resentment. Or just those damn hormones.

The door swung open, and there stood Fresno, leaning on the butt of a shotgun like it was a walking stick. He wore unlaced boots and not much else. His threadbare bathrobe draped open, exposing tufts of white-brown hair. He had the firm round gut of a great ape and a droopy wang that Zane did his best to ignore. "Hey, Fresno. How's it going?"

"Yeah, yeah." Fresno darted his scraggily head around and between them. "Okay. Get in here, Akron. Come on." Fresno tightened his eyes at Paul. "Make sure to lock that door behind you, kid."

Fresno leaned the double barrels against a coatrack, then led them down the front hallway. The air hung thick with the reek of unfiltered cigarettes, bacon grease, and patchouli.

The smell caused Zane's head to buzz. Or maybe he was just tired. Tired, and anxious for the white line's easy fix.

Behind him, Paul's voice broke low to high, like a bullfrog's. "Why'd he call you Akron?"

Fresno stopped and turned. "I call everyone by the town they come from." His red-eyed gaze landed on the kid. "What's your name, little brother?"

"Paul."

"Nah, man. I mean, what's your *real* name?"

"Oh, right." Paul nodded, very serious. "Albuquerque."

Fresno squinted. "Huh. I don't know. Makes me think of Bugs Bunny. Albu-coiky, Albu-coiky." He shrugged. "In your case, Paul, we'll make an exception."

They filed into the living room, where Fresno's girls sat on a slumping couch. They wore skimpy, faded dresses—prints of flowers and paisley—that draped along their slender hips and thighs.

Zane always forgot their names. Towns, of course. He nodded at the brunette and the redhead. "Ladies." They seemed like an incomplete set—like one of Charlie's Angels had gotten the axe. He imagined the want ad Fresno might post: "Old perv seeks blonde teen runaway for coke dealer harem." Zane didn't exactly relate to the whole Daddy vibe Fresno had with his girls. Then again, Fresno didn't seem like anyone's actual father. Zane's old man, for instance, was a miserable asshole, but he never paraded his dick around the house in front of kids. Not that Paul was a kid anymore. Or was he still? At fourteen, Zane had already gotten to third base with Katie Chernow. According to Saundra, Paul had never even held hands with a girl.

Fresno lowered himself into his tan Naugahyde La-Z-Boy and eased back into deep recline. He pointed at the brunette, her dark hair shining like raven wings. "So, Paul. This is Cheyenne. And that there... " He jutted his chin toward the oval-faced redhead. "That's Boise."

Zane and Paul sank into the cushions of a mismatched couch, opposite the girls. The kid waved at the girls, then looked away. His hands fidgeted in his lap, like a nervous old lady. These friendly, nubile chicks sat in front of Paul, and he wanted nothing to do with them. If Zane weren't so sure that the kid borrowed from his stack of old Playboys, he'd figure him for gay.

Boise tried to reel him in, nonetheless. Her voice all dusky with smoke, she said, "Pleased to meet you, Paul." She clamped a roach clip onto the butt of a lit joint and passed it to the kid.

Whenever Zane offered, Paul never accepted. But here he smiled at the pretty redhead. He popped that joint between his lips and slurped the smoke inside.

Something like pride bubbled up in Zane. "Hold it in, man." He smiled wide. "Hold it!"

Paul exploded into gasping coughs and sputters of smoke.

Zane laughed. "Yeah, well, it's a little harsh at first." But this was a rite of passage, on the path to manhood.

"Paul," said Cheyenne. "You have to breathe through your, like, Vishuddha chakra."

Zane gave Paul a couple of hard swats on the back. As far as CPR goes, that was all Zane knew.

"For Chrissake, Boise." Fresno said. "Fetch the boy a glass of water."

She glared at Fresno. "Fetch?" To Cheyenne, she hissed: "Why is it always me, fetching whatever needs to be fetched?" And she stomped into the kitchen.

Zane followed the riled-up sway of Boise's hips. Hey, when at the Gatehouse, do as Fresno does. And says.

After all that coughing, the kid looked a little wobbly, a little wrung out. When Boise bent down to hand Paul a glass of water, he didn't even peek down the front of her dress.

"Akron," Fresno said. "You got the time on you, man?"

Zane checked his watch. "Five 'til four." Then a nervous thought caused his chest to thump—like the deal might get postponed. "Why, you got somewhere to be?"

"Nah, man. It's almost time for Millionaire!" Fresno leaned forward. Eyebrows arched, he looked back and forth between Zane and Paul. "You know, *Who Wants to Be a Millionaire?* Shee-it, brothers. Greed, lifelines, that split-second divide between failure and success? That's America in a fucking nutshell. I consider it my patriotic duty to watch Millionaire." Fresno wrestled a remote control out from under his bathrobe, or possibly his bare ass. He aimed the clicker at the wall opposite his La-Z-Boy, and a wildlife show filled a giant TV screen. A cheetah dashed through clouds of dust and yellow grass, hot on the tail of some antelope or gazelle. "That's exactly what I'm talking about. Failure and success, life and death. It's all the same. But these animals, they're too pure for America. There's no greed. Only the instinct to survive."

"Yeah," Zane said. "I totally get it." He cleared his throat, just so he wouldn't seem too eager to change the subject. "So, before your show starts—"

Paul rose from the couch just then, and Zane followed the kid's sightline to a wide window that stretched behind the heads of the pretty girls. Paul edged around the coffee table, cutting in front of the TV just as the wiry cat leaped and clamped its jaws around its victim's neck.

Cheyenne smiled, sly and proud. "You see the stones, don't you, Paul?"

The kid nodded. "Ruins, right? I heard something about ruins." Paul looked over his shoulder, nodding at Zane with that wrinkled forehead of his. Zane knew the look. It meant Paul was impressed but also a little surprised that Zane hadn't made the whole thing up.

Zane shrugged and raised his palms. *Hey, not everything I say is total bullshit.* Then he turned toward Fresno, whose eyes tracked the bright flickers on the screen. "So, you said something about a fresh shipment from Columbia? I wouldn't mind sampling the merch—"

Fresno held his palm up at Zane. "That's right, kid. An ancient Indian temple." From the crevices of the La-Z-Boy, he excavated a bag of potato chips. "Where we're sitting right now? This used to be the entrance. The Gatehouse, I guess they called it." He tossed a fistful of chips into his mouth, then spoke through the crunch and mush: "Say, girls. Why don't you throw on some coats and show the kid around out there?"

Paul smiled wide for the first time in weeks. "That'd be awesome."

Fresno winked at Cheyenne. "She's gotten real good at giving the guided tour. Haven't you, baby?"

"Yeah, man. I'm, like, one-sixteenth Arapahoe? So, the Native land speaks to me."

Zane liked this idea. Send the kids out to play, and leave the men behind to snort and settle up.

Fresno crunched into another chip, then nodded his bushy head. "Now that I think about it … Akron, you should go along, too."

A series of aches rippled through Zane's chest. He laughed, tight and nervous. "You sure we can't just, you know, maybe finish up the deal right now?"

But the game show's opening sequence had begun. In disembodied voice, Fresno said, "Have a good trip." His eyes glowed wide in the swirling animations. He looked bewitched. Zombie-fied. His thumb lay into the volume button, and the show's bloated theme music blared across the living room.

Cheyenne stood and curled her long fingers, beckoning the others to follow her.

Zane groaned like an old man as he stood up from the couch. He joined the trek—through the kitchen and into the mudroom at the rear of the house. One door led to the garage, where Fresno had once shown Zane his stockpile of firearms, ammo, canned goods, bottled water, camping gear, and kerosene lamps. The whole survivalist kit and caboodle. The other door led to the great outdoors and that pile of old Indian rocks. Every time Zane had been out to the Gatehouse before, he'd managed to avoid the spooky chick's tour. Today, his number had been called.

"Seekers of mystery and truth." Cheyenne flung open the rear door, and a damp chill swept inside. "Follow me now, as we enter … the Lost Village."

ZANE'S BOOT HEELS sank into wet leaves and soaked earth. The thick mist crawled between bare trees, mossy boulders, and ferns. He buttoned up his sheepskin coat.

Cheyenne crouched by a weathered hunk of stone and waited for the others to gather around. "See those carvings? Those words are from the Salish tribe."

Mixed in with ordinary letters were strange symbols: $ʔ$ and x^w and $ə$. It looked like an inscrutable riddle, or maybe a tricky math equation. Zane hated both those things. They reminded him of the boring part of high school—the classroom part.

Cheyenne spoke the Indian words carved in the rock, her voice like a gust of wind. "In the Salish tongue, this means Lost Village." She stood, and her black hair shined with dew. "But who lost the Lost Village? The Indians? Or maybe they're the ones who found it. Could it be that the Aztecs journeyed north and built the Lost Village? Or maybe aliens from another planet got lost and landed here. We may never know for sure."

Zane's temples pulsed, and a tingle scratched at his throat. He didn't care much for history, either. What he wanted was whisky, then cocaine. No, cocaine and then a shot of whisky.

From his jacket pocket, he pulled out another toothpick, for chewing away the slow ticks of time.

"When tribal members entered the Lost Village, they would partake of a ritual smudging." Cheyenne stood before a large stone basin set atop a pedestal. She wrested a bundle of twigs from her coat pocket and lit them with a match.

The scent of sage lifted into Zane's hungry nostrils. Sage, and other pungent smells he couldn't quite place.

Cheyenne waved the burning smudge stick, and the bottom of the basin glowed. She pulled back her long hair in a fist, bent low, and dipped her face into the wisps of smoke. Then she moved aside. "Go ahead, Paul. Breathe it in."

The kid stepped forward and dunked his head into the basin.

A niggling apprehension pawed away at Zane. Toking on a joint was one thing, but … "Paul, maybe you shouldn't—"

But the kid had already inhaled hefty lungfuls. His eyelids fluttered, and he swayed in the rain.

Cheyenne sharpened her dark eyes at Boise. "Next?"

The redhead lowered her face over the bowl. "Mmm," she said. But Zane caught her breathing out—a foggy stream that slipped through her strawberry lips.

Cheyenne turned to Zane. "Your turn, Akron."

He detected a dare—a reminder of hangouts from his past. There was always somebody with a bottle, or a pipe, or a baggie, saying, "What are you, chicken?" But Zane had never backed down from a dare in his life. So he stepped up to the stone bowl and sniffed-sniffed into the smoke and glow. A rush of blood whirled through his head, and he wobbled in his boots.

"Now we enter the Great Temple of the Lost Village." Cheyenne's arms unfurled, wide as wings, and trails of iridescence swept across Zane's eyes.

"Oh, I'm so sure." In bubblegum-scented hisses, Boise whispered over Zane's shoulder. "This is the first I've heard of any Amazing Palace, or whatever."

Cheyenne yelled into the sky—a primal holler—and strode deeper into the woods. Paul, like a puppy dog, shuffled along behind.

Zane stood still, watching the forest swirl into new shapes, then back again. If he moved, he thought he might knock the world off-kilter. Man, what kind of insane Indian mojo had he inhaled, anyway? Psychedelics had never been Zane's drug of choice. Sometimes, he liked to downshift his mind with a bong hit or two. Other times, some lines of coke would throw his transmission into a higher gear. But acid, peyote, mushrooms? Whenever he took that shit, he drove right off the goddamn road.

Boise bumped her shoulder into his. "You just gonna stand there, or what?" Then she slid a fresh stick of pink gum onto her tongue and sauntered on.

Zane turned back toward the Gatehouse. The blue light of the television glowed in the windows. Dry air, soft couch. Phone a friend and cash winnings. He pictured white lines on the glass coffee table. He could almost feel himself floating back to that place. Then a hand tugged on his wrist. He wheeled around. But the others had left him behind.

Zane sifted through the woods, following Cheyenne's voice. Her speech came faster now, more erratic. He reached a clearing and found the dark-haired girl pacing a path into the mud before Boise and Paul.

"I mean, this must be it." Cheyenne pointed at a pair of Douglas firs, her pupils wide enough to crawl inside. "The whole story—how the Raven was hunted by the Wolves—it's right there, carved in stone."

Paul's jaw hung open He walked up to the trees, staring in wonder. Cheyenne had hypnotized the kid.

Zane felt pretty darn suggestible, too. Blinking into the silvery rain, he followed her long finger. Did he maybe see an archway made of stone? Animal shapes, like hieroglyphics, appeared. He doubted his eyes, his gut. In the Lost Village, Zane felt lost. "So, what are we looking at, again?"

"You don't know the legend?" Cheyenne frowned at Zane and shook her head, incredulous. "This is the entrance to Trickster's Labyrinth." Eyes squeezed shut, her hands did a slippery dance in the air. "It's the only place where Raven is safe from the Wolves." Step, step, turn. Step, step, turn. With each about face, her heels dug deeper into the ground. "And Raven … the Wolves have trapped her here, inside the Great Temple." Her eyes popped open. "Trapped. And I can't escape."

Boise leaned toward Zane. "Man, she's totally gone off the rails."

The redhead was right. Zane willed his head to clear, and the ancient structure bled away, leaving only the trunks of trees, red-brown and rough. Cheyenne was on a real bad trip. As the only adult present, was it up to Zane to intervene? "All right, folks. What say we head on back—"

"Shut up, Akron!" Cheyenne stopped and glared at Zane. "How do I know you ain't one of the Wolves?" The girl's expression grew fierce, wild. She turned to Boise. "Or you, bitch?"

"Cheyenne." Boise raised her hand like a crossing guard. "You totally need to just, like, chill out right now, okay?"

Even as Cheyenne reached inside her leather coat—and even as her lanky arm sprang toward him—the arrival of a sleek black revolver took Zane by surprise. The barrel was aimed at his face.

He threw up his hands and ducked sideways. He tripped. The ground swooped out from under him, and a whirl of browns and greens flashed through his eyes as he tumbled and slid, down to the bottom of a gully. Zane's skull thudded against something hard. Stone column, tree, whatever. Point being, it hurt.

The ground smelled of wood-rot and moss. A metallic tang coated his tongue. Zane pushed himself up onto his elbows. He spat red blood on green ivy. When he stood, his brain went cloudy for a second and a drizzle of vomit crawled up his throat. A part of him wanted to stay right there, hidden away from the nutso chick with the gun. But, if Paul got shot, Zane would be in the deepest shit of his life. So he clambered his way back to the top of the gully.

Boise lay curled on the ground, crying into a pile of leaves. Cheyenne had split. And where the hell was Paul?

Zane staggered forward. "Paul? Come on, man. We gotta vamoose!" He turned and searched, turned and searched. His aching head ached even harder. But no sign of the kid. "Okay, Boise. Pull your shit together. Where'd he go?"

She rose up to her knees, twigs and needles and mud all matted in her hair. "Amy." She snuffled and threw a stick at Zane. "My name is goddamn Amy, all right?"

"Sure thing." Zane wanted to be done with the girls and their mystical bullshit, done with Fresno, done with the Gatehouse. Done with cocaine? For the moment, the craving had disappeared. Near-death brought its own electric rush. Now he wanted only to return to Saundra. To wrestle his girlfriend into bed. To sweat out all the crap that coursed through his blood. To whisper in the dark, his skin pressed tight against her skin. He'd make new promises about how he'd change for her. But what if Zane returned home without Paul? All the promises in the world wouldn't amount to shit. Saundra would throw his ass in jail. "So. Amy. Do you know where the kid went, or don't you?"

"Cheyenne ran off that way." She pointed back to the passageway between the firs. "And Paul went after her. Into the Tricky Whatchamajigger."

Zane sighed. A bunch of damn trees, that's all. But the trees did seem to form some kind of passageway, so that's where he headed. Every dozen or so paces, Zane called Paul's name, and his own voice echoed back at him. The rain had stopped, but night fell fast. With two busted headlights, he couldn't drive home. Once he found Paul, they'd have to make their way back to the Gatehouse. Play nice with Fresno. Call Saundra and let her know her kid's okay. Then pass out on that pair of sagging couches and wait for the light of dawn.

The woods thickened. They tightened in around him. Zane zigged and zagged. "Paul! Come on, man." He stopped to listen. Nothing. He pictured the boy drifting further and further into the endless forest. Zane broke into a jog—an actual fucking jog. Each time his boot thumped the ground, a new ache rattled his skull. He kept one hand stretched out into the darkening world, halfway expecting his palm to scrape against the grit of stone. Instead, he touched only wet wood and tacky sap. His tongue hurt, his head throbbed, and his stomach cramped from hunger. But his thoughts had cleared. Unlike the mist. The mist held strong. "Paul!"

Zane bushwhacked, he stumbled, he cursed. Minutes or maybe hours later—who knew?—he found him. On the other side of a stout old redwood, a smudge of yellow cut through the night. The kid sat crouched on the pine needle floor, chin tucked, hood pulled tight over his head.

Zane stood in front of Paul, bent at the waist, gulping the hard, cold air. "Shit, I thought you'd maybe disappeared into some screwy alternate dimension."

Paul tilted his face up toward Zane. His cheeks burned rosy pink from the cold, or from crying, or both. "Me, too."

Zane reached down, palm open like a handshake. "Up and at 'em." That was one of Zane's dad's sayings. Every school morning, the old man would stand in Zane's bedroom door, clap his hands twice. "Up and at 'em," he'd bark. And,

"Let's hop to it." In his dingy bus driver's uniform, the old man had red-rimmed eyes and breath that stank of coffee and booze. Those handclaps must've pierced his dad's skull, every damn time.

Paul clasped Zane's hand and allowed his rag-doll body to be hoisted upright.

"Any sign of that crazy Cheyenne out here?"

"No." The darkness widened the kid's eyes. "She just, like, disappeared."

Zane snorted. "Figures."

"So, um." Paul looked all around, into the dense, wet woods. "How do we get out of here?"

Yes, the job of hatching a plan—that would fall to Zane. He didn't mind having to improvise his own escapes from life's booby traps. But now this sorry child-creature stood beside him, shivering in his stupid yellow sweatshirt. "Okay, this way."

Zane led them through the wide gaps between old-growth redwoods. He hoped to circle around that damn coyote's woodland maze. They walked in silence, looking for the glow of Fresno's television. Every hundred feet or so, Zane stopped and called out into the night. "Hello! Uh, Cheyenne? Amy? You still out here?" When they reached a clearing, Zane looked to the sky. The waxing moon turned the white mist whiter. But, even on a clear night, the constellations wouldn't guide his way. Zane had no knowledge of ancient science. Or modern science, for that matter.

He'd lived a life of picking up and moving on. Of rolling with the changes. He could always figure some way out of a jam. Now, by example, he would teach that skill to Paul.

He nodded at the kid. "A good night for camping, don't you think?"

Paul hugged his yellow arms across his chest. "We're totally screwed, aren't we?"

"Shit no. I've been through worse than this." He scanned the dim landscape. Fallen boughs littered the ground nearby. He envisioned the dry and sturdy lean-to they would build there in the forest. With toothpicks for kindling, Zane would teach the kid how to build a proper campfire—just like Zane's old man had promised to teach him.

Zane patted the pocket of his damp jeans and felt the outline of his Swiss Army knife. Finally, an object he could use. "No problemo." They would snare some wild game and roast the animal on a spit. A duck, maybe, or a squirrel. A squirrel? Whatever it took. They would eke out their survival through the night.

There Is a Tunnel

Kate sat at the beige vinyl card table that served as her desk. She'd nestled the table below an oblong window, where Danny had once slept in his twin bed, sprawled beneath a Star Wars bedspread. Only one year had passed since Jim took Danny back to New York. That meant Kate had wasted three years in San Diego—a place without weather, without temperature. Jim had tricked her into moving to California, then tricked her again into staying behind. No, that wasn't true. She'd tricked herself, both times.

Kate slipped the last Dos Equis from the six-pack that sat on the linoleum floor. The bottle sweated. The beer was warm on her tongue, in her throat. She stared out the oblong window, into summer's late morning glare.

Four orange trees huddled in the backyard of Kate's bungalow. From the plumes of waxy leaves and bright fruits, Marta Fernandez emerged. She carried a bundle of oranges in a basket made of her shirtfront. A hand-me-down from Kate's wardrobe, the plain white tee draped like a shift on tiny Marta. Housekeeper, gardener, cook, live-in maid—she possessed no identification, no possessions aside from the clothes she'd worn across the border. And her sketchbook, its pages filled with fluid pencil drawings of the people of Tijuana. Marta had appeared at Kate's front door six weeks prior, certain she had arrived at the right house. Certain that an underground passage had led her to that very spot.

A tunnel under the border. Marta must have been confused—disoriented by the arduous crossing, or possibly drugged. Kate pictured Marta in blue jeans and embroidered cotton blouse, her small body folded behind a false wall in the trunk of a dusty sedan. A claustrophobic terror. The experience must have *seemed* subterranean. Still, the idea tugged at Kate. In New York, she'd been a real reporter. She had chased real stories. Articles for the *Post*, the *Times*. Stories on Koch versus Cuomo, on the Son of Sam, on the burning of the Bronx. But she rarely slept. She drank martinis for lunch and missed dinners with her family. And then came the fainting incident, the intravenous fluids in the emergency room at Mount Sinai, and the ensuing "serious talk" with Jim concerning what would be best "for the whole family."

Now, Kate wrote a Real Estate column for the Homes section of the *San Diego Tribune*. She used small words to describe empty places. What did the word "home" even mean?

She sorted through memories of all the houses and apartments she'd lived in—with her parents, with college roommates, with boyfriends. Places she'd resided, nothing more. Maybe only the Brooklyn apartment had ever seemed like home to her. But that apartment, on the top floor and rent-controlled, belonged to Jim's family. Belonged to Jim. The San Diego house belonged to her. Level the place, for all she cared. But keep the orange trees. She felt calmest when tending to those four trees.

Beyond her backyard, beyond San Diego, beyond America, the world burned at its edges. Kate leaned toward the cathode warmth of the portable black-and-white television she kept in her office—in the room she still thought of as Danny's bedroom. She turned up the volume knob, as President Jimmy Carter announced the release of Richard Queen, the fourteenth hostage to be freed since the Iran

Crisis began, 250 days earlier. The news showed a still of Queen, with his jutting bearded jaw and his weary eyes—a deep fatigue framed by large, squarish glasses. Time lost in a strange land. Kate had not covered the Hostage Crisis. Nor had she covered Abscam, the Cuban refugees in Florida, the historic rates of inflation and unemployment. Nor had she written about Mexico's rising national debt and how poverty squeezed the lives of its citizens, leading to foreclosures, fractured families, desperate emigrants used as drug mules.

In the kitchen, Marta halved oranges on a wooden cutting board.

"Say, Marta. Tell me again." Kate smiled, hoping to soften her approach—her 'face of the Inquisition,' according to her ex-husband, the history teacher. "How did you get here? To America, I mean."

"Oh, sí." Marta tilted her head at Kate. "Um, cuál es la palabra?" One side of her face pinched together. "There is a tunnel. This is the right word?" She motioned with her hand—down, away, and up again.

"Yes." Kate swallowed the word and felt her hand go to her chest—a gesture she'd always thought phony when her mother made it. She dropped her arm back to her side. "So, truly? A tunnel beneath the border?"

"Sí, sí. Es verdad."

"Okay, hold on. Marta, did someone use you to smuggle … to bring cocaine into America?"

"La cocaína? No, no." Marta pursed her lips, shook her head. "Oh, no." She smiled, and her focus returned to the slicing of fruit. One, two, three oranges cleaved asunder.

"So, how did you find this tunnel?"

In Marta's hand, she held a perfect specimen—the yellow-orange of the sun, a bright sheen along its surface. "The Poet. He showed the tunnel to me."

"Sorry, wait." Kate shook her head. "The person who led you across the border, he was a poet?"

"*Sí*. I know him, but I never did hear his words before. But, when I am in the tunnel? He tells me a very good poem. And this poem, it takes me here. A su casa, señora Blaine."

Kate studied Marta's sweet face, aglow with the radiance of the converted, the saved. "And who is this poet?"

"His name, it is Manuel Roberto Dresner."

AT THE HEIGHT OF SUMMER, the Santa Ana winds carried a brittle heat across the city. The scents of citrus, wild aloe, and eucalyptus lightened the air, but the sun burned through all aromas. The flesh of fruit and the flesh of people darkened, toughened. Kate sat on the shaded wooden porch off the kitchen. Inside, Marta hummed a ranchera tune and swept the tile floors. Her story tugged at Kate. The possibility of a tunnel under the border—this riled up the old New York fervor, the reporter's hunger. Was this a newsworthy story? Kate still suspected that Marta had been drugged, and the tunnel was a fable she'd made herself believe.

Still, the tunnel called to Kate. Discovery, escape, return. The idea of the tunnel, itself—it grabbed at loose threads inside her. To plunge free of one realm and emerge in the next. To escape, and discover a new home. Or maybe rediscover an old home.

To find the tunnel, Kate would first have to find Manuel Roberto Dresner.

She prodded Marta for more details, but her responses only blurred Kate's comprehension. No, Marta didn't remember how she first met the Poet. Maybe Dresner had approached her? Yes, at her cousin Alonso's house, partygoers clustered into a cramped and muggy kitchen. She described Dresner as tall, strong, fair-skinned. She couldn't guess his age. The rest she knew only from rumors, but each rumor contradicted the last. Dresner was born in Chile. No, Argentina. He had fought in a war, or his father had escaped one. He tended bar, he worked for the CIA, he taught poetry at la

Universidad. In exchange for Marta's private exodus across the border, had Dresner asked for payment or favors? No, Marta insisted, he had not.

Kate began her investigation at San Diego State's Department of Chicano Studies. A professor there recognized Dresner's name, but intimated that his work belonged outside the movement, somehow. "Oh, right," the professor said. "The South American. The German." UCSD library's Baja California collection offered no sign of Dresner until 1977, after which his poems appeared here and there—in a journal from Tijuana, in a small-press anthology out of Los Angeles. The librarians all shook their heads. Dead ends. Then a fellow patron emerged from the nearby stacks. He had overheard Kate's query. He knew of a certain bookstore.

At Biblio Barrio, in a dusty stack of periodicals, Kate unearthed three mimeographed and hand-stapled volumes of *Las Poemas Mezquinas*, a bilingual journal from Ciudad Juárez, edited by Dresner. Spring, Summer, and Fall of 1978. Kate brought these to the front counter, to a narrow-faced old man who wore his silver hair combed back with pomade. He leafed through the Spring issue, nodding. "Manuel Roberto Dresner."

At hearing a stranger's voice speak his full name, Kate's shoulders roiled with a shiver. Whether from fright or thrill, she couldn't tell. Maybe she reacted to the rhythm of the Tria Nomina. Lee Harvey Oswald, Mark David Chapman, James Earl Ray, John Wayne Gacy. The American mind: conditioned to associate fear to a man's full name.

The bookseller set the chapbook down on the burnished wood counter. "You know his work?"

"No, not yet."

The bookseller smiled. "Well, you will. He did more than edit these collections. At least half of the poems here are Dresner's own. He used many false names."

"Oh?"

"But he won't tell me which are his."

"So …." Kate blinked at the old man. "You know him, then?"

"Oh, yes. He stays sometimes at a house two doors down from my own. A house of wanderers—musicians, artists, fellow poets. Latino youths. Whenever Dresner appears, they loan him the use of an old couch. It's a sagging disaster, left to molder on the back porch." The old man chuckled. "But the Poet never seems to mind."

BARRIO LOGAN WAS A neighborhood of small proud houses and outsize murals. Portraits in bold colors, formed of swirls and waves. The vibrancy of lives arisen. At summer's end, strong beams of gold light streamed across Chicano Park. Pull-tabs from soda cans glinted along the fissured sidewalk and cigarette butts filled the gutters. A sea-brine tang hung in the air, mixed with the musk of brackish water, carbon monoxide, and rancid corn oil. Beneath a brick red awning, a pair of caramel-skinned women cradled infants to their chests and laughed into the warm evening sky.

Kate shaded her eyes and scouted the storefronts for signs of the meeting place. Her destination was a taqueria, or maybe a cantina.

A month earlier, she'd looked for Dresner at the address given to her by the owner of Biblio Barrio. A young man with shaggy black hair had sat on the stoop, scratching words into a notebook with a tight-gripped pen. She'd asked for the Poet, and the nickname drew a soft laugh from the kid. He hadn't seen Manuel in a while, but he would pass along her name and number. Weeks later, Dresner called Kate to set the meeting place. She'd told him only that she was a writer and wanted to meet him. "Esquivel's, Friday, five o'clock," he'd said. She'd interviewed men like him before—decisive, ritual-bound. There would be no negotiation. She could simply agree or refuse.

Esquivel's was dimly lit, its walls the color of smoked salmon. From a transistor radio propped on an orange crate, a Spanish guitar swayed through melancholy lines, while a mescal-voiced woman pleaded for mercy from the specter of sorrow. At least, that's how Kate interpreted the song. She found a booth in the back corner and called out for a Dos Equis. A girl in a pretty peach dress brought tortilla chips, fresh salsa, and the beer. The girl looked underage, barely past her quinceañera. The owner's daughter, probably. Kate had intruded upon a community centered on the idea of family. Meanwhile, her own family had drifted apart, in glacial shards. Her parents divorced when she was ten. Her younger brother—nominally a tour guide—lived on a Florida key to which he claimed no phone service ran. It didn't matter. The Blaines had always evinced disdain at connection, at contact.

Kate took a swig of beer, brown bottle to thin pink lips. She wore no lipstick, no eye shadow. She pulled back her straw-blonde hair with a plain metal barrette. Beige linen capri pants, cornflower blue gingham shirt, white boat shoes scuffed and streaked from treading the loamy soil beneath her orange trees. She wanted to present a neutral front. Sexless.

From her daypack, she dug out a yellow legal pad and blue Bic pen and laid them on the table. She rummaged deeper and found the Autumn issue of *Las Poemas Mezquinas*—*The Shabby Poems*, as the introduction informed its readership. Kate flipped to an entry by Juan Vargas, entitled "Los Perros" on the verso, and translated as "The Dogs" on the recto. She'd convinced herself that she'd ferreted out Dresner's style and that he had penned that poem. Or, possibly, as both editor and translator, Dresner's style had seeped into the English versions—the only versions that Kate could fully comprehend.

He walked in then. Dresner. Kate hadn't been able to dredge up a photo, but he stood out anyway. He was tall enough, as Marta had said, but only compared to the average Mexican. His high cheekbones betrayed the vestiges of a Bavarian severity. Running through his mud-brown hair were the rust tones of the Patagonian Desert.

In long, sure strides, Dresner approached. "Kate Blaine," he said, then sat across from her. His greeting had posed no question. He needed no confirmation. In Barrio Logan, she stood out even more than he, and pleasantries clearly bored him. Would she bore him, too?

"Yes. Thanks for—"

Dresner turned his head away and raised a finger to the young waitress. He caught her eye easily enough. Dresner glanced at Kate and arched his eyebrows—the hint of a question.

Kate nodded, without knowing what she'd just assented to.

Dresner held up a second finger. "Dos," he said.

The girl spun around and bounced back into the kitchen.

Dresner was handsome, yes. But Kate sought to submerge those low bodily wants. It was her spirit that hungered. "Thanks for meeting me."

He tapped out a cigarette from the pack he kept in the breast pocket of his off-white guayabera shirt. Dresner lit up, took a long drag, and slid home the pack of cigarettes. "You're a reporter."

"No. Well, yes. But not right now. That's not why I'm here." Kate surprised herself with that statement. She thought she had come to investigate a story. With or without her probing, knowledge of the tunnel would eventually surface because stories wanted to be known. And she, too, wanted to be known—known as someone other than a Real Estate columnist. Someone better. But her true needs ran deeper, tangled in the roots of belonging. Where did she belong? And who did she belong to?

Kate felt his eyes on her. The heat of observation, of being observed—this heat rose to her cheeks.

The girl set their drinks on the table, then flitted away. Clear plastic juice glasses, two fingers of tequila in each.

"You have a reporter's eyes," he said. His voice was low and clear, an accent betrayed by a light roll of the r's. "But they're not a poet's eyes, I don't think."

Kate looked down into the shallow well of amber liquid. "I don't know what that means." She tried to conjure an image of her own narrow face, of her pale blue eyes—her *ice blue* eyes, as Jim had noted more than once. "But you might be right." She shrugged, then forced herself to raise her chin, to meet the flat gaze of Dresner's hazel eyes. "Actually," Kate said. "A mutual friend prompted me to find you. Marta Fernandez."

"Ah, Marta." He inhaled from his cigarette, and his attention widened—a look of active remembrance. "So." Dresner flung back his tequila and gulped it down—a move so swift that it startled Kate. He winced at the liquor's sting, but in a way that conveyed deep pleasure. "The tunnel, then."

Manuel Dresner had blurted out the word, but Kate felt the need to shelter the secret they revealed. Elbows on the table, she leaned forward. "The tunnel. Yes."

AT THE SAN YSIDRO BORDER CROSSING, the lanes of traffic fanned out wide. Up ahead stood the checkpoint. Beyond, Tijuana's great and ominous maw. It fed on row after row of cars. The vehicles slipped into the gullet of Mexico like prescription pills, coated in shiny sugar-shells of midnight blue, burgundy, and school bus yellow-orange. In the dusk-haze, the checkpoint's lights glowed, diffuse and portentous. Banks of bright white lights, like at a baseball field. Further on, indicators at each check station changed from red to green, green to red. The colors of Mexico.

A reporter on the radio announced that Iraq had invaded neighboring Iran. Saddam Hussein tested the will of Khomeini to govern the nation he'd so recently seized.

"This will be the news now." Dresner lit a cigarette. He stared ahead at the line of cars as he spoke. "Two days ago, the Sandinistas assassinated Somoza. The end of three generations of C.I.A.-sponsored despotic rule in Nicaragua. Do you journalists deem this as newsworthy? Barely, if at all. And why? Because the lives of fifty-two American hostages are not at stake. Also, Nicaragua has no oil reserves. The United States is indifferent to the Latino experience. Until, of course, it bleeds across the border."

Kate sighed. But not out of empathy for the Latino plight, as she hoped Dresner might think. Kate sighed out of disappointment in herself. That skirmish in the Middle East marked another missed opportunity, another story beyond her reach.

Dresner raised a finger from the steering wheel, gesturing ahead. "The day workers, and their cycle of exile. Spat out each morning from their own nation. And every night they are banished once again."

The Mexicans' cars mixed with the Americans'—the revelers and the whoremongers, youth in their thrum, old men with bets on bullfights, married couples questing the exotic spark. Among these, who was Kate? Another stupid blonde turista. That, she thought, is what they'll say when they find her body—raped, mutilated, and dumped into an arroyo.

"This was a mistake." The tequila swayed through her brain, but the statement felt clearheaded.

Dresner blew smoke out the window of his battered Ford pickup.

Kate watched the slow crawl of the processional. But she sensed his eyes on her.

"In my head, I'm writing the poem for you," he said. "The one you will need to find your way across."

She turned toward him. "Across?" A staccato laugh—plosive, incredulous. "Wait, wait."

"Marta explained it to you, I'm sure." He lifted his foot off the brake, and the pickup eased forward, slotting closer. Ahead, the shit-brown border station loomed. "And this is the experience you crave, am I right? You can't just *admire* the tunnel, you know. It's not some ride at Disneyland." His lips curled. An incisor, chipped and yellowed, snagged on the soft, dry flesh. "That's not why the tunnel exists."

Their turn came. A uniformed man extended his hand from a window.

Leave now, Kate thought. As a mother, wasn't she obliged to follow safer paths, to remain steadfast even in absentia? She should pry open the pickup's door and walk back through the field of headlights. Away from the mouth of Mexico. Maybe America was a good mother, after all. Her arms lay open wide, beckoning her own children back to her bosom.

But Kate didn't open the passenger side door. She felt an itch inside, at the cellular level, that told her to stay. And continuing seemed inevitable. All the forces at play— Manuel Dresner, the spread of twilight, Tijuana's phantasmic glare—those forces drew her forward. She sifted through her daypack, while the two men watched her, doomed to their impatience. The guard had already returned Dresner's papers to him. She felt the thin edges of her billfold on her fingertips, its middle bulge against her palm. Kate stripped her driver's license from its clear plastic sleeve and stretched her arm past Dresner's face. He stared ahead—bored, or content, or consumed by interior maneuvers. Did that blunt expression hide the soft corners of a churning mind? Did pretty and ferocious words bloom inside his brain and struggle into sweet arrangement?

The guard nodded, and they entered the southern land.

FOURTEEN YEARS EARLIER, Kate and Jim had honeymooned in San Diego, sowing the seed for their future transcontinental migration. The newlyweds, in a rented convertible, had day-tripped to Tijuana. A small city back then, lively and bright. The trill of Mariachi in the languorous air, souvenirs too cheap to carry back with them to New York. They had a delightful day. When dusk began to spread, they crossed the border back into California. They'd watched *Touch of Evil* together at a second run cinema, and Jim wanted to shield Kate from the city's nocturnal depravations.

The Tijuana of 1980 startled her, and Kate felt an inkling of fear. Dresner drove them down the freeway, and the glare of the city's half-million souls burned everywhere around them.

"The tunnel," Kate said. "How many people have you—?"

"Not many." He crushed the tip of his cigarette into the truck's ashtray.

They passed billboards for jai alai tickets, currency exchange, Tecate.

"So, why Marta?"

Dresner steered them off the highway and onto a wide boulevard. "Mexico wasn't her true home. I could see this. Her family—Marta told me—she didn't belong to them."

"Well, I can certainly understand that sentiment."

"Sure. This idea, it's the heart of the American philosophy. Individualism. But, for a Mexican—for any Latino anywhere—to feel apart from the family is to be afflicted with a faulty spirit. Most Mexicans who cross the border? They leave in order to make money for their families, back on the other side. It's a communal mentality."

In downtown Tijuana, faces shone lurid in the neon light. Gringos and locals alike spilled off the sidewalks and into the streets. Storefronts overlapped, crowding each other out. Plywood signs, blocky words stenciled in competing tongues, advertised: "Best Prices!" and "Joyería Oro y Plata!"

"So, okay. Wait." Kate squeezed her eyes shut. "You singled out Marta *because* she was unlike other Mexicans? Because she placed her own needs ahead of her family's?"

"If you've read my poems, then you know that they are portraits of the individual. Not a family, or a country, or a lineage of traditions that connect the Spaniards to the New World. Maybe this perspective was passed down through my German blood. The narrow lens of my miserable father, and my miserable grandfather before him. Or maybe it's simply that I belong to nowhere."

Not belonging, yes.

Kate had dragged herself from one coast to the other, and she'd left some crucial element behind. She'd cleaved her own soul. No, that had occurred years before, decades before. A congenital defect, maybe. The genetic marker for Cleaved Soul Syndrome fizzled amidst the strands of the Blaine family DNA. Jim was right to abandon California, to bring Danny with him back to New York. Back to his old school friends, back to Jim's sister and parents—the nurturing branch of Danny's family tree. Because the move to San Diego hadn't been "for the whole family." They'd uprooted themselves entirely for Kate's sake. They'd found a place to calm her nerves, to dry her thirst. Okay, maybe she should have sold the bungalow and followed Jim and Danny back East. Instead, she'd allowed her family to leave her behind.

"So, yes," Dresner said. "I possess a very un-Latin perspective. And Marta shares this perspective. She sees the world through the artist's eyes."

Kate nodded. "Her sketchbook."

In front of a pawn shop, a young couple strolled—hips locked, hands in the back pockets of each other's jeans. Her feathered hair draped across the spaghetti straps of her halter top, and he smiled wide beneath his thin, dark mustache. Kate wanted to watch them forever, to follow that couple to whatever bar or bedroom awaited them that night. To pursue the lives of others and escape her own.

Dresner pulled through the intersection, and the couple vanished into the pulse of the avenida.

"Marta showed me one of her portraits," Dresner said. "Drawn with an everyday pencil in simple lines. A portrait of Padre Juan Guerrero, the scoliotic old priest from the neighborhood church. La Iglesia de Nuestra Señora de Guadalupe. It's a pathetic structure, and he's a pathetic man. But Marta, she revealed a great beauty in his sad gray eyes. Not as a window *to* his soul, as the lousy poets say, but as a reflection *of* his soul. That shitty little church, it was the old man's cathedral. And you could see this from the way that Marta drew his eyes."

The business district bled into the barrios. At the roadside, vendors sat huddled under streetlights. Straw sombreros overran their wooden carts. Fringed serapes lay draped over clotheslines strung between beat-up Impalas and rusted LeSabres.

From the bulevar, Dresner turned the truck onto a narrow calle, its asphalt busted and crumbling into dusty shoulders. The rich, warm scent of fresh tortillas invaded the pickup's cabin. Acid gurgled in Kate's gut. Since lunch, she'd consumed only beer, tequila, and a handful of chips. The slalom of the small street wobbled her equilibrium. A sense of unease—both airy and leaden—suffused her skull. She shut her eyes and fought against a sick and sleepy drift.

"Okay, then," Kate said. "I suppose I understand why you led Marta to the tunnel. But why me?"

"Ah, the real question." The Poet grinned. "Curiosity, I think."

"Curiosity. What are you curious about?"

"You are curious about the tunnel. And I am curious to see what the tunnel will reveal to someone like you."

"Oh, someone like me?" Kate sighed. "Okay. Wonderful."

Her jaw clamped and her arms crossed tight. The involuntary sulk. *Someone like me.* Dilettante, WASP, the divorcée with ice blue eyes. And through her eyes, the city unraveled. A time-lapse film of decay, poverty as a physical force. Its hot momentum thumped against Kate's chest. She wriggled her jaw loose, unwound her limbs. *Someone like me.* The Manhattanite, the prep school snob. Raised by a pack of socialites. In a single night, the Blaines could spend on dinner and a Broadway show what this entire shanty region could spend in a week on groceries, rent, diapers, cigarettes. *Someone like me.* Kate knew where she'd come from, who she'd been. But she couldn't envision who she might become. Could she return to her old self, maybe? A new version of her old self.

She closed her eyes, weary of the jostle and the scorn. Her body yearned to cocoon itself beneath Danny's Star Wars bedspread. A discarded artifact, outgrown by her son. The blanket now sat tucked into the top draw drawer of Kate's filing cabinet. The smell of Danny lingered in its weave.

KATE BLINKED HER EYES OPEN. Manuel Dresner, the old pickup truck, Tijuana. Even awake, she couldn't have mapped their trajectory. Still, she felt angry at herself for having lost the thread of their travels. The stupid Americana, dragged into the middle of nowhere. Her limbs tensed, alive once more to the danger of the unknown.

Dresner swung off the paved street and onto a dirt road. They rumbled over potholes, and dust gathered like fog in the headlights. Grit crawled between Kate's teeth. On the black hills, the outlines of tiny houses sat in a landslide array. The neighborhood teemed with activity. The sounds of trumpets and vihuelas filled the night air. Music came from a thousand radios. Rancheras, corridos, norteños. The sway, the blare, the joyful sorrow.

"This is Colonia Altiplano." Dresner raised his chin. "Where Marta used to live. And where I call home."

Large families loitered in front of their plaster houses. Doors precariously hinged, windows wedged into irregular geometries. Chickens grilled over outdoor fire pits. The peel of children in mad zigzags throughout the barrio. They laughed like drunkards, exuberant from their own exuberance. Had Danny sprinted and whooped like this in San Diego? In Brooklyn, he had. White kids, black kids, a blur of T-shirts and tennis shoes—the little madmen of the neighborhood.

At the corner of a bustling block sat a makeshift bodega of corrugated tin, a large Pepsi logo over the door. Kate's skin buzzed with the body's steep needs: water, food. But she didn't ask Dresner to stop. She'd given herself over.

They turned and drove, cresting tight curves, shimmying down single lanes. Fewer Mexicans walked the streets here. A quietude pervaded. Patches of scrub grass sprouted from the barren earth. They had come to the edge of the sprawling city, and only the chaparral stretched beyond. At the end of a hushed road, between two dilapidated houses, Dresner glided his pickup into a small driveway. "This is it," he said.

Kate had to lean her shoulder against the door of the truck before it budged. She swung out her legs—the muscles heavy and cramped—and slid down to the hard dirt. She snatched her daypack from the cab and pushed her arms between its straps. Dresner waited, a flashlight's beam aimed up the gravel drive. Kate clambered over a toppled pile of worn tires. Her ankle turned, and she barked a sharp exhalation. He didn't seem to hear her.

They walked, wordless, up the steep drive. The rough macadam shifted and crunched beneath their footfalls. Lit only by a slivered moon and distant specks of stars, Dresner's face held cryptic shadows—they rendered him even less scrutable. Kate's heartbeat leapt into a gallop, and the sharp pain in her ankle blossomed into a warm throb.

They came to a small cinder block building, the spare desert-land all around. Far away, a highway sighed and moaned. The building bore a single metal door, a blistered rectangle of white adhered to its surface. The old sign's message had been erased long ago by exposure to the unforgiving sun and air. All former warnings and cautions would go unheeded.

Dresner slipped a key into a padlock and clicked it into release. The door opened without a creak. Every unexpected detail like this grabbed at Kate's lungs. *Breathe*, she told herself. *Remember to breathe.*

Inside, Dresner pulled a cord, and a bare bulb illuminated the earth-scented chamber. A cylinder of mortared stone, thigh-high and maybe four feet in diameter, rose from the center of the small room's dirt floor. A thick metal lid lay across the top of the stone structure.

In front of Kate's feet, a tarantula scuttled past and crouched in a corner, its hairy legs poised. Kate pressed her hands flat to her chest. Her breath burst from her lungs. The black-eyed creature shook loose all the dormant terror that lay inside her. Why the hell had she come to this place? "Oh," she said. "Oh, I don't know."

"Well." Dresner sighed out his nostrils, like a steed, or a bull. "See what you think, anyway."

Kate could neither imagine retreating from that spot, nor pressing on. She allowed the momentum of the journey decide for her. She nodded, and her hair swam loose at her temples. With quick sweeps of her fingertips, she pushed the fallen strands behind her ears.

Dresner threw a bolt and heaved open the metal lid. His face reddened with the effort, and a clenched grunt escaped him. The lid clanged to the ground.

Kate leaned over the low stone ledge. The beam of Dresner's flashlight lit the circular pit. Bolted to its surface, a steel ladder ran down to an unknown depth—beyond the light's reach. "A well?" she said.

"Something like that. Who can say? Now, it's the origin of the tunnel."

Kate ran through the possibilities: a mine shaft, a missile silo, a defunded cistern for use by the local fire department, a maintenance entrance for a subway line that never existed. She returned to her original assessment—a dry well. The simple idea brought her a small comfort. "I can't see the bottom." She watched his face for signs of how she might feel.

"No, you can't see the entrance of the tunnel, but it's down there." Dresner glanced at her, then returned his gaze to the dark subterranea. "The tunnel maintains its own mystery. To descend is an act of faith." He nodded. "Yes, faith is the first step."

Kate swiped her palms down her face, her fingertips passing over her soft-shut eyes and along the contours of her cheeks. Through the pliant gateways of flesh, blood communed with blood. Her heartbeat spoke, from everywhere inside her. Primordial and true.

"Okay," she said.

"Good. And your poem is ready, too. I'll recite the words as you climb down. I call it a poem, but it's more like an incantation. Words from the tunnel, itself. Like a spirit guide, like a map."

Kate had trained her thoughts onto the physical obstacles before her. Notions of mysteries and incantations, these slipped clean past her.

She climbed onto the edge of the well, perched in a low squat over the ladder's top rung. "And you'll meet me on the other side?"

He looked up from the gloaming, his hazel eyes dilated in the dim room. Dresner handed his flashlight to Kate. "The other side, yes."

Her right foot found a thin rung, and then her left foot landed on the rung below that. Her ankle ached, and she exhaled the pain in short, sharp breaths—like blowing out candles, or preparing for childbirth. Kate clenched the flashlight in a circle made of index finger and thumb. Her free fingers, she wrapped around the ladder's cool metal rods. The cone of light danced along the rock wall, below.

Dresner's voice—low and sonorous, with its Latin lilt—followed her down. "You drink the hot blue sky, but its juices fail to quench your thirst."

The words passed through her. *Sky, juices.* The climb consumed her mind. The tunnel, she hoped, would listen on her behalf.

"Parched and apart, pasts and futures push you aside. Sunlight dances through your hair, but your eyes are unlit moons."

She scaled down into the old well, its musty years suspended in the cooling air. *Moons, eyes.* She imagined twin spheres of barren rock in subzero space-spin. What had she expected from Manuel Roberto Dresner—a fond farewell?

"Below the soil of the great Sonora, your eyes seek to illuminate. To witness the lines you must transgress. You leave your home, and you leave your home, and you leave your home again."

Kate halted her descent and tilted her head back. The world above dissolved into haze—dim light, soft edges, all aura. Only Dresner's voice remained firm, a steady stream. *Leave, home.* Yes, and always on the search for home. And wasn't this the Poet's story, too? Itinerant, a wanderer by nature. A person of parched needs. And, if they shared this great lack—this separation from life's wet heart—then maybe Dresner would protect her, would guide her, would reveal the tunnel to her.

She tightened her left hand's grip on the ladder, fanning the flashlight's beam below. The floor of the well remained elusive. It swallowed the light. Down she climbed.

"A desert's journey to slake a thirst. In the labyrinth of Baja, you quest the straight line, the etched-out truth, the homebound way."

The air closed in around her. Dry throat, depleted stomach. Kate's head grew hot, her thoughts diffuse and rustling with dream-stuff. In the barren well, she saw Jim and Danny in the old Brooklyn house, lanky limbs at the breakfast table. And she smelled the bright tang of oranges, tasted their warm nectar. Commingled senses. One home, another home. Where was home?

"Will you find your way?"

High above, the sky boomed. The metal lid slammed shut.

Kate's heart stopped mid-beat, stuck against her chest. Fear rippled through her mind. Dresner had imprisoned her, abandoned her. Did this make sense? No, this must be the plan. Yes, a repetition of Marta's own journey through the tunnel. He needed to leave Kate in order to drive back across the border, to meet her at the tunnel's terminus. He'd merely left the well protected, the tunnel hidden. The stricture in her ribs shook loose. She wasn't trapped. Of course not. The entrance to the tunnel lay just below.

Down the sightline of her hip and leg, Kate followed the flash's dancing beam. The light appeared to skim across a new geometry, there in the stonework—a glimpse of shadowed edges and planes. The cool depths chilled her hands, but a fresh heat prickled her forehead and cheeks. She paused and closed her eyes. Yes, she could feel her feet and hands on the ladder's rungs. She was fully there, in the well. Kate opened her eyes and felt the sting of trickling sweat. She aimed the flashlight down. Was that a break in the wall?

Dresner had commended faith, and now something like faith stirred inside her. She believed in the tunnel. Just as Mexico had drawn her toward its aperture, now the tunnel would lead her home. Kate would fulfill the cycle. She would return, faithful and resolute. But return to where? To Danny, somehow? Would the tunnel lead Kate to her son? Or would the passage carry her back to the San Diego bungalow, with her four orange trees and her live-in housekeeper? With faith in herself, could she make that house a home?

Kate drew a long, slow breath. Her lungs expanded—to purify and to sustain. The air passed through her lips. The prickling heat, it gentled and spread, enwrapping the whole of her body. She felt suspended. Held. Safe as a newborn. No, safer still. Safe as the pre-born, floating free in the amniotic world.

Kate climbed further down—one step, two—her motions light and easy on the iron rungs.

Worry and indecision melted into the auric warmth. Kate turned off the flashlight. She didn't need it anymore. The bottom of the well beckoned, welcoming and near. She felt the presence of the tunnel, its entrance at her back. She heard its heartbeat hymnal, low and strong as a mother's pulse. The life-giving flow. Kate's own heartbeat had once nurtured the bones and eyes and lungs of the baby cocooned inside her. And all those years before, her mother's blood had sheltered Kate, aswim in the womb.

She slipped one foot off the lowest rung and stretched her leg down, arms straining, hands gripping tight and pointed toes reaching, reaching for the ground at the bottom of the well. She shut her eyes, in surrender to the heart-pulse of renewal, the breath of rebirth. Kate's fingers loosened their hold. She was ready now, for whatever lay below.

Orange Valley, White Valley

a novella

Chapter 1

2022

The U-Haul rattles on the washboard ruts as it climbs Lilac Lane. The shaking is familiar to my bones, though I haven't been on this road—aside from one other time—in the last forty years. Not since Mom sped us away from my childhood home.

Now I'm back in Orange Valley, and everything looks the same. Except, nothing is the same. My father is no longer alive.

Dead. My dad is dead. I should feel something, shouldn't I? Sorrow, anger, grief, regret, a great unburdening? But all my emotions are wound up tight, like the layers of yarn inside a baseball. I can't get through the outer hide, much less down to the hardened core. All I know is to keep moving forward.

At the crest of the hill, late afternoon sunlight blasts through the windshield. Squinting beneath the visor, I see it below: the old farmhouse. Really, our family's property isn't much of a farm. Just a three-bedroom ranch house, a garage, and a chicken coop I suspect my father left to the weeds. But the land itself is starkly beautiful. Five acres of Southern California chaparral: wild yellow grass, sage brush, dry earth, and a grove of slender eucalyptus trees where Eduardo Ayala's white trailer once sat. A gully with a shallow stream cuts a verdant scar down the heart of the property. On the far side of the gully is a wide-open field. In this light, the yellow grass looks like golden wheat. I remember its gentle sway.

I also remember, at age thirteen, the view from my bedroom window on a particular night. A patch of that tall grass, illuminated by flashlight and the silhouette of a man working a shovel in the deepest dark. That was the night Eduardo vanished from Orange Valley. And, quite possibly, the living world.

My heart bounces like a ball against the wall of my chest. I brake and throw the truck in park, right in the middle of the road. The lurch wakes up Griffey, my white lab, who's curled beside me on the black vinyl bench seat. She looks at me with expectant brown eyes, waiting on my next move. But I can't move.

Griffey's paws scuffle on the truck's slick seat and she gives me a little whimper. *Come on,* the sound says, *I have to pee.*

"I know. Me, too."

I hope the county didn't shut off the water before my payment cleared. Likewise, electric and cable. And the mortuary. So many bills, so much paperwork, so many phone calls. What a pain in the ass. I'm sure Dad's smirking up at me right now.

I throw the truck back into drive and ease down the hill. Off to the right, where a large avocado grove once stood, the land has been subdivided. I feel disoriented as I pass newly built homes with xeriscaped yards and shiny SUVs parked in the driveway. Suburbia has invaded the rural landscape of my youth. To my left are the green waxy leaves of orange trees. The familiar sight is a relief. I wonder if the Prochazkas still own this grove that runs along the southern border of our property.

Well, I guess it's just my property now. My sister, Melissa, doesn't want anything to do with the place. She lives in

Denver, has a husband and two kids, works part-time for a non-profit, and keeps an eye on Mom, who's in assisted living there.

I don't especially *want* the property, either. But I need a place to live, and Dad paid off the mortgage on the farm years ago. As an accountant, the one thing he did right was take care of money.

As I maneuver the U-Haul down the dirt driveway, I feel disembodied, stuck between times. I'm used to sitting in the backseat and staring at my parent's heads. My ex-Army father wore his russet-brown hair short by the standards of Southern California in the 1970s and early '80s. Mom, by the end of our time here, had transitioned from long, straight, dishwater-blonde hippie hair to dyed-gold Farrah feathers that whisked her shoulders. I inherited Mom's naturally plain hair color, Dad's bulky torso and gray-blue eyes, and the weakest facial features of each—though I like to believe my beard disguises my squishy jawline. Well, it's not just my face. At fifty-three years old, I've gotten soft all over.

I pull up in front of the decrepit ranch house I've inherited and turn off the van. On the day we left my father behind, the paint was brick red with white trim. Now the colors are faded-bloodstain and ancient bone. Mom's rosebushes are dead and gone, leaving a barren patch of dirt out front. On the other side of the driveway, the vegetable garden of forty years ago is now a rectangle of weeds. Farther along is the barn-like garage, where a gutter hangs loose. Already, a to-do list scrawls itself across my brain. Item number one: pick up Dad's Buick LeSabre from the tow yard. A headache threatens my skull.

I heave open the cabin door. My cramped legs unfold, my dead-stiff spine crackles. When the soles of my shoes hit the dirt, there's something about the surface tension, the texture, that feels like home. As does the snap-dry air of late spring.

The sense of comfort is disconcerting. I'm not ready to feel at home here. Not yet.

Griffey bounds from the truck, trots over to the nothing yard, and squats to pee. By the time I've climbed the two steps onto the wooden front porch, my dog is at my side. She's an eager participant in whatever journey I might undertake. I wish I possessed even half her enthusiasm.

I pull out the house key—one of the few personal items Dad had on him when he collapsed at the Orange Valley Speed Mart and was taken by ambulance to the hospital one town over.

Three weeks ago, when they called to inform me that my father had passed away, I should have reached out to my sister. Or possibly Mom. Instead, the first person I called was my ex-wife, Sheila. She knew better than anyone how I felt about the man. "I just found out he's dead," I told her. "And I already feel like he's haunting me." Sheila snorted over the phone. "Doug," she said. "You've always been haunted by your past. For as long as I've known you, anyway. And that's a long damn time."

The screen door opens with a whine, just as it always has. Or had the hinges only started to complain during the last couple of years I lived here? The shitty years, the drunk Dad years, the falling apart years. Maybe all the years of my childhood had been like that, or had been gradually degrading, entropy building, the breaking point looming ever closer.

As I open the front door, the house's stench knocks my head back. In the living room, there's dust on every surface, sagging couch cushions, a jagged crack in the glass-topped coffee table. Memories hit me hard—so many darting scenes that I can't sort through them, can't judge them as good or bad. They clog up in my throat. They crash into my ribs. My friends and I used to sit cross-legged on this same swamp-colored shag carpet playing Atari games in front of a walrus-sized TV, where a flat screen now stands. And I used to hide at the end of the hallway there, watching my father pace this same stretch of floor, highball glass in hand, snarling mustache-mouth running off a litany of complaints to Mom: against her, against the neighbors, against his business partner, against the immigrants, against the Natives, against the government, against the world.

Griffey brushes past me, white tail wagging and black nose lowered to the filthy carpet, cruising the living room like a runaway vacuum cleaner, snorfing up smells. Apparently, the rank and musty odors don't bother her one bit.

I consider calling her back to me. Turning around. Locking the door. Driving away. Selling the place as is. Buying a one-bedroom somewhere cheap: Idaho or Iowa or Illinois. Anywhere near a baseball club that I could write about. Somewhere I could scrape together enough freelance gigs to pay for groceries and utilities.

Griffey scoots around the corner, down the hall. I exhale a pent-up breath. Then I follow, flinging open windows along the way.

I swing open the first door on the right. Melissa's childhood bedroom. She was eleven when we left. Even though she relocated all her possessions—Duran Duran posters, pink bedspread—to our new house in Denver, I expect to find them here, the space unchanged. But our father has filled the room with towering stacks of magazines and newspapers. I'm standing between columns of *Field & Stream* and the *San Diego Tribune*. The room vaguely resembles an art installation, some confused commentary on urban life and the state of journalism. To be sure, Dad frequently ranted about both.

Was I merely rebelling against him when I moved to a big city and worked for a newspaper? Well, he got the last laugh there, I guess. My long-running tenure as a sportswriter at one of Seattle's venerable papers ended with its purchase by some infotainment media conglomerate. I was hardly singled out. A third of the staff were made redundant. Then the pandemic hit, and Sheila got laid off, too. Our marriage at its end, I moved into the remodeled basement. Neither of us could afford to live alone—especially not while still paying our son's out-of-state tuition. Now Ben's degree has landed him a web design job in Silicon Valley. And Sheila's shacked up with a new guy, in a condo downtown.

Meanwhile, I'm back in the boonies again. At least I'll have time to write. There's a book I've been outlining for the past twenty years. So far, all I've settled on is a title: *Bad Hops: The Greatest Baseball Players Who Never Were*. My plan is to profile maybe a dozen guys from different generations, all of whom seemed destined for Big League stardom until, for one reason or another, their careers imploded.

I move on to the next room, my old bedroom, where I find Griffey nosing around a labyrinth of aluminum table legs. The legs support a pair of craft tables pushed together. Sitting atop is what appears to be a large-scale diorama. It reminds me of a deluxe model railroad setup. Except, instead of a little train station and maybe some quaint New England buildings and autumnal trees, Dad's diorama features a row of shacks along a muddy delta, a dense tropical jungle, six tiny die-cast U.S. Army figurines, and maybe a dozen villagers. I feel like I recognize the place from my father's oft-told tale of his final day in action. *When a goddamn Gook shot me in the leg.*

The American soldiers advance upon the village, rifles raised. A squadron? A platoon? Dad would be dismayed that I don't know the difference. The villagers seem to be in the midst of everyday activities: child-rearing, gardening, and the like. Though their bodies are positioned at a variety of angles—crouched this way, leaning that—every villager's head is pivoted toward the invading force. The moment of irreconcilable change.

Just looking at the diorama, my skin tightens all over. My lungs clutch. There's something eerie about it I don't understand. I sense the pieces moving, feel the vibration of a collective pulse. But then I focus hard on a particular villager—a woman with her hand raised before her face, as if to shade her eyes against the sun or to ward off what's coming—and her figurine remains perfectly still. Inert.

Must be the fatigue. Last night, while staying at my son's apartment in Santa Clara, I dreamed of Eduardo Ayala. We were standing in an orange grove. He spoke to me in rapid Spanish, desperate to relay some kind of message, but I could barely parse his words. My high school studies from thirty-five years ago have mostly eroded. I woke up with a gasp, sweating in a strange bed, and couldn't fall back asleep.

I turn away from the diorama and walk quickly from the room. Griffey trots out alongside me. I shut the door. Tight.

Across the hall, I stand for a while, breath calming, and stare blankly into my parents' bedroom. Dad's bedroom, I guess. He's the only one who's regularly slept in here for the past forty years. As far as I know. The air in this room is particularly malodorous: a stale funk of old man whiskey-sweat, humid leather shoes, and a lifetime of cigarette smoke. The bedsheets are rumpled, and a shallow concavity runs along one side of the mattress.

I fling open more windows. Through a torn screen, a black fly hurriedly buzzes in, as if it had been waiting in line for ages outside a popular nightclub. More bugs are sure to follow. Honey bees, red ants, mosquitoes.

"Come one, come all! This haunted fucking house is yours!"

Hurling the words from my chest feels good, but reality sets in quickly. What was I thinking? No way am I moving to Iowa. And I don't want to get bitten and stung all night long. I slam the window shut over the ripped screen. Then I grab an issue of *Popular Mechanics* from the nightstand, roll it tight, stalk the fly until it lands on the same shut window, and smack it dead with a sure-and-easy swing. Just like hitting fungos to the infielders when I used to coach Little League.

Used to. No longer. Another piece of myself I lost to the pandemic. Other people seem to have recovered their broken pieces, fit them back together to form new and sometimes more beautiful stained-glass lives. All my pieces lie scattered at my feet, jagged side up.

Griffey lays her snout on my thigh, and I realize I'm sitting on the edge of my father's bed. When did that happen? I squeeze my eyes shut, press my fingertips over the lids. I rub my palms down my face. The contours surprise me. I'd expected, for a moment there, to feel my smooth, thin, thirteen-year-old face. Instead, my palms cup the bulk of decades accumulated, the coarseness of a graying beard.

I stand up, turn, and face Dad's bed again. No way in hell am I sleeping on that thing. But evening's coming on, and I don't have it in me to drag in my mattress from—as I now recall—the very back of the U-Haul van. It's the couch for me then. Or the bench seat in the truck. Or, hell, now that I'm living in Southern California again, I could just camp out under the stars.

I head back down the hall, though the living room, and into the dining room. It's far from formal. The same grimy orange linoleum covering its floor wraps around into the big country kitchen. The two spaces are divided by a long, high countertop bar. On this side, three rattan stools stand at the bar, looking forlorn. Dad used to sit at one of those very same stools—the middle, usually—and harangue Mom while she cooked dinner or washed dishes.

Windows run along two walls of the dining room. I open every one, hoping to let the foul air out and the eucalyptus-scented air in. Through the west-facing windows, the smoldering orange of sunset bleeds through the branches of oak trees. To the north, across the gulley, lies the wide field of yellow grass where I once watched my father dig Eduardo Ayala's grave.

That isn't necessarily true, though, is it? Having gone to journalism school, I should know better than to conflate supposition with fact. And I've waged this argument with myself a thousand times. I've interrogated my younger self—the boy who witnessed shadow-shapes from a distance, who made deductions based on eavesdropped words and the sudden absence of an itinerant, undocumented man.

Exhaustion hits me in the chest. The weight of memories. The days of driving a rumbling truck down the length of the Pacific Coast. And everything else on top of that. Everything, everything, everything.

I drag myself into the kitchen. It looks mostly the same. How depressing. How reassuring. The beige fridge—didn't my folks buy that thing the year before we left? Whatever rotten food it harbors, I'll confront that horror tomorrow.

Out the kitchen door, I head to the U-Haul and grab a bag of Griffey's dog food and the six-pack of beer I picked up at the liquor store—one of maybe a dozen storefronts in all of downtown Orange Valley. When I showed the clerk my ID, he gave me a curious squint. He must've recognized the Lundvall family name. For many decades, my father, Nick Lundvall, was a regular customer there.

Back in the kitchen, I pop open a beer using the bottle opener that's mounted to the underside of the counter. How many Cokes and Orange Fantas did I liberate in the same way throughout my childhood?

Thirteen years I lived in this house. An onslaught of curses and lies.

Griffey noses the back of my knee.

"Sorry, sweetheart." I find some plastic bowls, fill one with water and the other with kibble, and set them in a corner of the dining room. I drop into a chair, sip my beer, and watch the sunset's slow darkening. The sharp edges of my nerves go rounder, softer. With each mouthful, I'm less and less tempted to turn my head to the north, to face the field of pale grass. Tomorrow, I tell myself. Though I still don't know exactly where or how I'll pass the night.

Bap-bap-bap! The sound is a shock, heart-pausing. Griffey stops her chomping, looks up, growls uncertainly. Someone knocking at the screen door, I realize. Who the hell, at this hour? I suck in a breath. "Just a sec!"

As I shuffle through the living room, the person standing on the other side of the screen door takes shape. A woman's contours. A familiarity to the sharp angle of her jaw, the slope of her narrow nose. A face like a fox's. Just how I remember the neighbor girl. Only I didn't remember her being so pretty.

"Leslie Prochazka?"

"Hey, Doug." She opens the door and lets herself in. "Thought I saw a U-Haul turn down the driveway here. I was worried some Silicon Valley jackasses might be moving in."

"Nope. Just me. A familiar jackass, anyway." I feel a stretching at my cheeks, as if I might be smiling.

"Well, that I can handle." Leslie grins, drawing out the crow's feet around her dark brown eyes. Her waves of sandy hair have gone partly gray. She's dressed in worn-out jeans and a plain tan tee. No makeup, no jewelry. She looks as if she's been out working among the oranges. A scent of citrus lifts off her.

"Come in," I say pointlessly. "Get you a drink?"

"Sounds good," she says, and follows me into the dining room.

"That's Griffey," I say, as my neighbor rubs my dog's floppy ears. "Beer?" I hold up my bottle.

"Whenever I popped by to check on your dad, he usually served whiskey. Any of that around?"

"Oh. Well, thanks for doing that." I'm trying to imagine Leslie sitting at this battered oak table, drinking with my father. Having goddamn conversations with the man. Wait, what had she asked? Flummoxed, I just stand there, looking everywhere and nowhere, as if a drink might emerge from the stagnant air.

Leslie heads straight for the sideboard, extracts a fifth of Jack and one of Dad's highballs, and pours herself a thumbful. Then she pulls out a chair—her regular chair?—and settles in.

"Sorry to hear about your dad." She leans forward as she says this, eyes gently locked on mine.

I see it now, the resemblance to her mother. As a boy, I had a crush on Sue Prochazka.

"Thanks," I remember to say. There are sentiments I'm meant to add, I believe. Instead, I take a drink, just the right amount of bitterness on my tongue. "Honestly, I still don't know how to feel about it. About him."

Leslie makes a face I can't untangle—part smile, part frown. Sympathy? Irony? Kindness? Pity?

"That old bastard," she says. "I don't blame you. I'd have mixed feelings, too. Hell, my dad's still with us—if barely—and I already feel conflicted about him dying. Part of me wishes he'd just go ahead already. The other part is like, 'No, Daddy, don't abandon me!'" She chuckles. "Pathetic, isn't it?"

"No. Course not."

Her smile looks tired. "So. Back home, eh? After, what, decades away?"

I snort-laugh, as if Leslie's told a real zinger, an absurdist punchline. "Yeah, I guess I am."

She nods, nurses her whiskey.

Being near her again feels oddly natural. Though she's essentially a stranger, Leslie reminds me of the goodness in this place. She was the sweet, innocent kid who lived next door. Then again, a whole lot of years have accumulated since I saw her last.

"What about you?" I say. "Been here in Orange Valley all this time?"

Her face squeezes into a frown. "Hell no. I left for college when I was eighteen. Didn't move back until three years ago, when it looked like the business might otherwise collapse."

"Left for good and came back anyway? I can relate." Part of me wants to know what's happened to the orange grove next door. The other part is exhausted from thinking about property and aging parents and pressing finances. "What did you do in between?"

"Got a couple of degrees, taught agriculture at Cal State Fresno, married a sociology professor." Leslie narrows her eyes at me. "Doug, never marry a soc professor."

"Ha. No, huh?"

"Divorced his cheating ass back in 2016. Same year we elected a pussy-grabber for president. What a world!" Leslie throws back the rest of her whiskey and plunks the glass on the tabletop.

The dining room has gone dusky. I stand up, flick on the light, then nearly fall back into my chair. The brass fixture suspended above the table casts a yellow glow over Leslie and me. Reflections of the dining room fill the windowpanes. Now that I can no longer see the outside world, its mysteries start rooting around my chest, scratching to come out. I feel Leslie's eyes on me.

"You remember Eduardo Ayala?" I ask.

"Sure." She sips her whiskey. "He worked for us for a while. Then my dad fired him. Said he was lazy, did a bad job, some crap like that."

"You believe him?"

"I don't know." Her head tilts, as if she might better read the past this angle. "I remember, around that time, a big summit meeting between your folks and mine. Looking back, I think something more personal was involved."

"Me, too." I could expound on that idea, but I want Leslie's take. My own notions have been piling up inside my skull for ages now. They can stay put a while longer. "So what do you think made Eduardo disappear so suddenly?"

She shrugs. "I always assumed they reported Eduardo to border patrol. Figured he got snatched up and sent back to Mexico."

"Yeah, could be." I take a long drink of beer while I deliberate my next words. For now, my deepest suspicions feel too tender, too wild, to expose. But Leslie has a right to know that she was used as ammunition. No, more like bait. "That, uh, summit meeting you mentioned? I was there that day. I overheard what our parents said."

Her fine eyebrows dart up. "And what was that?"

Chapter 2

1982

Dad had instructed Melissa and me to "get lost for a while." Apparently, he and Mom had an important matter to discuss with our neighbors, the Prochazkas.

I'd called my one friend who lived within walking distance, but the line had been busy, so I'd trudged the half-mile up to his house. I stood on the porch, knocked at the front door, waited. The summer sun baked into the back of my neck. Knocked again, waited some more. A drop of sweat streaked down from my temple to my jaw. Clearly, no one was home.

Turning on the heels of my Pumas, I started down the gravel driveway, back toward home. I dialed up the volume on my handheld silver transistor radio. A Sunday afternoon, and the Padres were playing the Giants. As I jogged across the shimmering asphalt surface of Valley Grade Road, the radio's tiny speaker crackled with a burst of cheers from the crowd. My brain lit up, imagining Terry Kennedy's home run ball clearing the outfield fence. Maybe, by the time I got home, the talk with the Prochazkas would be done, and I could watch the last couple of innings on TV.

I cut through the Hinkleys' avocado grove. The scalding air cooled a few degrees, sunlight flickering through dark branches, thick leaves, and the fruits with their green, puckered skins. My thoughts bled into the sounds of the ballgame.

As I veered between two trees, I nearly ran into Eduardo. That year before my growth spurt, he had a couple of inches on me, along with plenty of hard-earned muscle that filled out his faded denim shirt. In addition to working for the Prochazkas, Eduardo did odd jobs for us in exchange for living in a small trailer on our land.

"Ai!" He laughed and danced aside. A beam of sunlight glanced off his enormous belt buckle—a brass oval depicting a cowboy riding a bucking bronco. "Sorry, Doug."

"No problem."

Though Eduardo wore cowhide gloves, his fingers moved nimbly as he inspected the avocados.

I asked him, "You working here now, too?"

"Sí, Señor Hinkley, he give me the job." A sad smile crept onto Eduardo's proud face. "Because, well, Señor Prochazka … I do not work for him now."

"Oh, okay." I wanted to tell him I was sorry, but I had only a tenuous understanding of the situation. Was Eduardo fired or did he quit? Either way, maybe the change was for the best. Tomas Prochazka had a gruff demeanor and stern dark eyes that rattled me. Whereas the Hinkleys, whose house lay far enough away from our own that I rarely saw them, seemed pleasant enough. As employers, they had to be preferable to either Mr. Prochazka or my father. Dad often found excuses to snap at Eduardo, to cut him down.

"What is the game?" Eduardo pointed to my radio.

"Padres and Giants."

"Ah, sí. No Dodgers, eh? No Fernando?" He grinned, knowing that I knew that he didn't care too much about American baseball, except when Mexican pitcher Fernando Valenzuela was on the mound. On the occasions when Fernando pitched against the Padres, I would find Eduardo and we'd listen together while he picked fruit or mended a fence.

"Next week, I think they play each other."

"Okay, Doug."

With half a wave, I left Eduardo and continued my trek through the avocado grove. Later, our near collision would become a snapshot moment I'd hold onto and re-examine. It would be the last time I'd see Eduardo in the waking world.

By the time I reached Lilac Lane, the inning was over and a car salesman was barking from the radio. I slipped the volume low.

While trudging alongside the Prochazkas' orange grove, I heard the thin and jittery sound of a pop song blaring. It sounded like another transistor radio, maybe even the same budget Sears model as my own. I followed the brittle beat down a row of trees, the bittersweet scent of orange blossoms enveloping me. The song kicked into the chorus, and a girl's voice joined in, mumble-singing the phone number of some-one named Jenny. I zig-zagged a couple of rows over and onto the thin strip of lawn that bordered the Prochazka family's yellow ranch house. Leslie sat cross-legged on a bench on the front porch, radio propped up at her side. Their house was the same vintage as our place, but better cared for.

At eleven years old, Leslie was a beanpole in brown cor-duroy shorts and a checkered shirt, a youthful shine to her bowl-cut blondish hair. Two years her senior, I saw her as a child still. Though my sister was just one year older than Leslie, Melissa already looked and behaved like a teenager. In her Jordache jeans and pastel tops, Melissa had ruled sixth grade at Orange Valley Middle School. She referred to Leslie as a country bumpkin. I didn't think much about those kinds of distinctions, then or now.

Leslie was twisting the rows of a Rubik's Cube, making the colors align.

"Hey," I called out.

"Oh. Hi, Doug." She smiled, guileless and wide.

"Your folks still over at my house?"

"I think so." Leslie shrugged, then craned her head back over the Rubik's Cube and continued humming along to Tommy Tutone.

"All right. See ya." I turned and headed back into the grove.

Another commonplace interaction, even more innocuous than the last. Later, I would cling to it as well: a document of my precarious little world as it reached its tipping point.

From the orderly matrix of orange trees, I emerged onto our property and hiked down the ragged slope, toward the rear of the detached garage. On a flat rock in the middle of my path, a brown and scaly horned toad lizard sunned itself. The creature tilted up its head as the baseball announcer's voice returned. The next inning was underway, but I clicked off the radio. If my and Leslie's parents were having this long of a conversation, then the topic might be intriguing. I wanted to eavesdrop on the goings-on of the adult world.

I snuck around the garage, dead grass brushing my bare shins, and jogged across the turnaround at the end of the long dirt driveway. As I made my way along the back of our house, I ducked beneath open windows. Through the screens, adult voices carried. Sharp words, an argument. I couldn't make out the specifics, but I could discern Mr. Prochazka's light accent among them. And I could tell from the trajectory of speech that everyone was in the dining room.

I headed for the row of manzanita bushes, which bordered a flagstone path that ran alongside the gully. Over the years, the dense bushes had become overgrown and unruly. As I'd learned, they provided an excellent hiding spot from which to spy. I crouched in seclusion, not ten feet from the dining room's array of open windows. I had a clear view of everyone gathered around the table. My parents sat on one side, Sue and Tomas Prochazka on the other. The women's profiles were nearest to me.

"Because." Tomas said. "The man is a pervert!" From my angle, I couldn't make out his expression, but could readily imagine his dark-eyed stare.

"But why?" Mom's words carried clearly through the hot summer air. Her heart-shaped face turned from Tomas to Sue and back again. When neither responded right away, she raised her palms, her habitual gesture when confronted with a lack of disclosure. "What did he say? What did he do?"

And which man? My brain flicked through the faces I knew in Orange Valley—neighbors, teachers, school bus driver, postman, cafe owner, Dad's business partner—like searching through baseball cards for a specific player. Was one of these men a pervert?

Dad leaned back in his chair, its front legs lifting an inch or two from the orange linoleum. He pulled a Marlboro from his thin lips, huffed gray smoke toward the ceiling.

"Yes, it's what he did," Tomas said. When he glanced at his wife, Sue looked out the window. Right toward me. But her worried blue eyes didn't seem to register my presence.

The beautiful Mrs. Prochazka. She had an oval face, delicate features, a slender yet shapely figure that caused my head to buzz. I would sometimes find her tending the trees nearest to our property line, and her beauty would knock me into paralysis. Watching her out among the oranges, she always seemed so sure of herself. Not now.

"Our daughter," Tomas continued. He rubbed a hand over his forehead and through his fine salt-and-pepper hair. He wore his usual outfit of crisp, dark blue jeans, cowboy boots, and checkered shirt tucked in. "He brought out his thing in front of our Leslie."

The legs of my father's chair banged to the floor. Dad stood, chest out and shoulders back—a posture ingrained from his Army days, though he hadn't served in well over a decade. "Oh-ho-ho!" he said, a sneer on his lips. "That fucking figures, doesn't it? Goddamn animals, every single one of 'em."

Mom's head snapped up at him. Though she was turned away from me now, I knew the glare she was giving him. When company was over, she found Dad's racism far less tolerable.

I realized, then, that the man they were discussing wasn't white, which ruled out most everyone I knew in town. Aside from Eduardo, of course. Even my thirteen-year-old brain could connect those dots. *Señor Prochazka … I do not work for him now*. Tomas had fired Eduardo for flashing Leslie. Allegedly.

Mom reached a hand across the table, her fingertips resting millimeters away from Sue's wrist. "Is that what happened?"

"Goddamnit, Maria." Dad frowned at Mom while pointing at Tomas. "The man just said so!"

Sue Prochazka focused on my mother's face, her eyes watery and beleaguered. Her pretty lips opened. She spoke so softly that I held my breath, straining to listen. "What I remember … I think …" She cleared her throat, and her voice lifted. "It was night. I'd gone outside, to the back of the house. I don't remember why. A noise?" She glanced at her husband. "Yes, there must have been a strange noise. And Eduardo was there, near Leslie's bedroom window." She paused again, the muscles in her face taut, like rubber bands pulled to their limits. "Leslie was asleep, but she could have woken up at any time. She could have seen, but she didn't. Thank god."

"And I," Tomas said. "I had noticed Sue's absence. By the time I got there, the bastard was stuffing his thing back in his pants. I fired him on the spot!" Tomas slapped the tabletop. "Told him never to return."

"Ha!" Dad laughed. "See, Maria?"

Tomas sat up straighter, smiling proudly. He gave his wife a pat on the hand.

I didn't fully grasp condescension at that age, the cruelty inherent in certain kinds of praise. Still, the scene imprinted itself on my memory. I would call it up many times over the years, revisiting the words and gestures through an adult lens. Had Sue Prochazka done her husband's bidding and lied about Eduardo? Or had she merely pleased Tomas by admitting the awful truth? Why, then, had she looked so unwilling to relate the incident? Was it a regretful truth? Or a regretful lie? All these questions I'd ask myself later. In the moment, I was merely a stunned observer.

"Oh, Eduardo." Dad shook his head. "You dipshit. You really did it this time." He paced the dining room with his hobbled stride, cowboy boots thumping the linoleum. He took angry drags off his cigarette, expelling smoke with purpose. The others watched him intently. Dad had a way of gaining power through sheer momentum, as if accumulating static electricity. At any moment, sparks might fly.

"Will you do it, then?" Tomas said. "Fire him as well? Remove him from your land? We want him as far away as possible."

I glanced over my shoulder. Between the cool-gray trunks of eucalyptus trees, I could just make out a glinting corner of his old white trailer. It was a crappy little home, but all he had.

Dad stopped, turned to face the table. A tight smile crawled up his lips. "Oh, I'll remove him, all right. I'll make sure he's good and gone."

DESPITE DAD'S PROCLAMATION, Eduardo didn't vanish right away. It took a few days. My father had to work himself up to it, I think. As usual, he riled his energies by fighting with Mom.

Harsh voices had pulled me out of bed and down the dark hall, toward the living room. Melissa already stood at the far end of the hall, barefoot, in a pink oversized sleeping shirt. As I drew near, she turned and held a shadowy finger to her lips.

"No, Nick," Mom whispered. "Like I keep telling you, I don't believe a word they said."

I watched my parents over Melissa's shoulder. Mom sat perched on the arm of the La-Z-Boy, the cuffs of her lilac pants flaring over the mud-green shag. The drink in her hand looked pale, mostly melted ice. Dad stood maybe six feet away, one arm leaning on the fireplace mantel, the other supporting a highball, his whiskey dark and neat as a slap.

"Oh, come on." His throat sounded scratchy, his words bitter. He swirled his drink. "Tommy the Polack seemed pretty damned sure of himself."

"Jesus. He's Czechoslovakian, and you know it."

This fight seemed more important, the stakes higher, than the usual topics they argued over. Mom's paltry income as a rookie real estate agent, Dad's drunken laziness on the weekends, meddling in-laws, mealtime snits, forgotten promises. I thought of Dad's earlier vow: *Oh, I'll remove him, all right.*

"Well, wherever he's from," he muttered. "The point is, that fucking Mexican pulled out his dick in front of their little girl."

My little sister's hand flew up to her mouth, muting her gasp. She was too young, I thought, to be overhearing this discussion. So was I. The whole thing made my stomach hurt.

"Or so Tomas says." Mom's eyebrows arched and tugged. "I think they're covering for Sue. I've seen the ways she and Eduardo look at each other. Secret smiles."

Dad erupted into laughter, and Mom shushed him. "*Secret smiles*, Maria? For shit's sake. Too many romance novels for you."

"I don't read those. Don't you even know me at all?"

"I know what I see." Dad nodded, a sour kink to his lips. "And it's you who's always flirting with that Mexican Romeo. Standing too close. The little laughs and sighs. What, you thought I hadn't noticed? Well, ha-ha-ha, Maria. I've noticed, all right. And I've let it slide for too damn long." He pushed off from the mantle, took two loping steps to loom over Mom, who did her best to hide a flinch. "Now I'm fucking sick of it. Eduardo is done here."

Chapter 3

2022

I keep dreaming about Eduardo Ayala. Over the past couple of weeks, since moving back to Orange Valley, he's appeared to me several times, always amid the orange trees. In these dreams, orderly groves transform into hedge mazes pocked with lurid orbs. Is it me or Eduardo who's trapped inside? I can never figure it out. Worry lines streak his amiable face—the otherwise smooth face of a young man, frozen in his prime. I've gotten better at deciphering Eduardo's urgent Spanish phrases. Each time, more words follow me from my sleep. I type them into my notes app, translate them more efficiently each time. Still, the results are imperfect.

In last night's dream, Eduardo stood in a corner of the labyrinth grove, an overripe orange like a dying star balanced in his palm as he told me:

I am, I am from, I am. Falling is like the earth. I spin, you see.

I'm certain of the first sentence: Soy, soy de, soy. But what did this declaration of selfhood mean? And where had Eduardo come from? The rest, I may have butchered. Was it *tierra* for *earth*, as in dirt? Or had he meant *Tierra*, as in the planet *Earth*?

I set my phone down on the nightstand, which, for many decades, was my father's nightstand. Though I'm sleeping where his bed once lay, the box spring, mattress, and linens are all mine. I've also changed out the art on the walls. Gone are the motel-quality abstractions of steelhead trout, vintage pickup trucks, lonely trees. In their place, I've hung my own forms of art: a black and white print of Mt. Adams taken by Ben during a recent father-son hike, a signed team photo of the Seattle Mariners from 2001. That was the year they won 116 games and reached the playoffs. Ben turned one that autumn, and the Twin Towers fell.

America's hastening decline is yet another reason to drop out of life, to dissolve into the chaparral. But what have I escaped? This house is a form of purgatory, a place where restless spirits dwell. And maybe I'm like Dante, only a tourist here.

I force myself to rise from bed, to plant my feet on the shaggy floor, to begin another day. Griffey springs up, wags her tail. As we head toward the kitchen for our breakfasts, I wonder: If I'm Dante, then who is my Virgil? The yellow lab bumping against my leg? Instead, it's Leslie's face that swoops across my mind. Tender blood rushes to my heart.

I KNOCK ON THE Prochazkas' door. They've kept the exterior in good shape, Leslie and her dad. I'm envious. Fresh coat of yellow paint, no loose boards on the porch, the white bench still standing after all these years. As the door swings open, I half expect eleven-year-old Leslie to answer. Each time we've talked since my return, her adult face surprises me. A good kind of surprise.

"Hey there." Her smile is warm. She's pinned up her hair and put on a pretty sundress for our Saturday lunch date, or whatever this is. Her doddering father will be joining us, so my expectations are low.

"Hello." I hold up my offerings—a clump of geraniums from the one bush Dad managed not to kill and a bottle of lemonade I concocted myself, from the lemons in my own front yard. "You look great."

Leslie takes the bottle and bouquet from my hands and, with an easy tilt of the head, invites me in. "I'll put these in some water," she says, and leaves me to look around.

The living room is tasteful: hardwood floors, matching furniture without any visible cigarette burns, shelves plump with books. Have I ever stepped foot inside the Prochazka home before? Though neighbors for years, our families rarely mingled.

A voice from behind me: "Nick Lundvall?"

Hearing my father's name sends ice water down my veins. I turn to find an old man in the next room, sitting at the dining room table. I would swear he's dressed in the same checkered shirt he wore forty years ago, when he manipulated my father into getting rid of Eduardo. And what if Tomas contributed more directly to Eduardo's disappearance?

"No, Dad." Leslie emerges from the kitchen. At the center of the table, she sets down a tapered glass vase, my red geraniums arranged neatly within. "That's Nick's son, Doug." Then she turns and leaves me to my own devices.

"Oh!" Tomas Prochazka gazes at me, his eyes wide and mouth slack.

I can't tell whether his mind has gone slate-blank or is cranking furiously through computations. In my years as a sports reporter, I would occasionally find myself in the same room as one of the team owners, a man whom I remembered having met before, but whose dubious squint informed me that I'd failed to make an impression on that important individual's discerning brain. Deciding to handle Leslie's dad like an oblivious team owner, I stride over to his end of the table, smile politely, and extend my arm for a handshake.

"Good to see you again, Tomas."

His knobby hand loosely clasps mine. His silver eyebrows remain pinched, but the stupefaction in his expression has eased into mild skepticism. Which is exactly how I recall him having looked every time I saw him, half his lifetime ago.

And the majority of my own lifetime. In some ways, though, I feel as if the intervening decades never occurred. Like I'd dreamed the failed marriage, the cut-short career, the rambling Seattle home where Sheila and I raised our son.

Leslie returns from the kitchen with a plate of deviled eggs.

"Help you with anything in there?" I ask.

She gives me a small, knowing grin. "No, I'm good. Have a seat. You two get reacquainted while I finish up."

I settle into a chair and angle myself obliquely toward Leslie's dad, so that we aren't staring at one another.

"So…" I don't know how to begin the conversation. I already know how he's spent the majority of the last four decades: growing and selling oranges. And I already know that his wife, Sue, died of cancer a dozen years ago. And I'm pretty sure he's caused his beautiful daughter no small amount of heartache throughout her life. Should I ask him what he watches on TV? Does he even remember?

Tomas's eyes flick my way. His thin lips move in a silent rhythm, as if the words in his brain run on separate tracks from their formation in his mouth. So many rails and switches, with fewer in commission every day, I'd imagine. And yet I suspect, somewhere inside that balding head of his, Leslie's dad knows exactly what happened to Eduardo. If I only I could climb inside that wrinkly dome, I'd search every compartment for the truth.

"You are visiting your father?" Tomas's Czech accent is thicker than I remembered, confusing my sense of time and place, as if his dementia might be catching.

"Oh, no. My dad died a few weeks back."

He's scowling now. Maybe he doesn't believe me. His frown is so intensely furrowed, I disbelieve myself for a moment. My father isn't dead. He can't be. He still owes me—what, love and respect? Or, at least, some hard truths.

"Sorry." Tomas says this as if he'd bumped my shoulder in passing, the word weightless in the air.

"Well." I feel my facial muscles constrict, a scratching in my sinuses. My throat jams up. Apparently, I'm holding back tears. I hadn't realized they were coming. Goddamnit, Dad. I inhale a deep breath, and words sigh out of me: "I guess I'm your new neighbor now, Tomas. Maybe for good."

When I look up, Leslie is standing alongside the table, opposite me, a platter of hot dogs and buns in her hands. Her deep brown eyes hold me, steadfast. A smile nudges her lips. "Is that right?"

I'M WALKING ALONGSIDE Leslie as she gives me a tour of her orange grove. A home care worker is with her dad right now, so we have the afternoon to ourselves. It's a warm Sunday, and Leslie looks especially pretty—carefree and light—in a pastel skirt and blouse, pink-painted toenails peeking through her sandals. The trees are neatly aligned, like the rows and columns of stats on the backs of baseball cards. The sky is hazy, the brightness soft on our eyes, soft on the green waxy leaves surrounding us. The fruits themselves look a shade paler, by and large, than they did a month ago, when I first came back to town. I mention this to Leslie.

"June is getting a little late in the season," she says. "The deeper orange color comes from the cooler nighttime air in fall, winter, and spring."

"What variety of oranges do you grow?" Though I lived next-door to her family's oranges my entire childhood, I never learned a damn thing about them. Now I feel like I should be scribbling notes, recording her answers. I have to keep reminding myself that I won't be writing an article later. I'm just learning more about the woman beside me—how she spends her days, how she sees her world.

"Just the one cultivar," Leslie says. "The Washington Navel. It's perfectly adapted for California's more arid climate. Florida oranges are good for juicing, but these are the best oranges for eating." She twists free a particularly ripe specimen and, smiling, hands it to me.

With my thumbnail, I slice into the rind. A mist of sharp-sweet tang hits the air. I start peeling the orange into broken curves, tossing the pieces to the earth below.

"Navels travel better, too. See that white part of the skin?" We slow to a quiet halt. On the half-naked fruit, Leslie's fingertip hovers near to mine. "That's the albedo. It's thicker on the Washington navel than on other oranges, giving it some extra padding."

"Okay, so, why the name? Do they come from Washington State?" Just picturing it, my skin can almost feel the damp chill of the territory I recently called home.

"No, from Brazil, actually. In the 1800s, the USDA got hold of some navel trees. They got named for Washington, D.C. Then along came Eliza Tibbets. This is the 1870s. Eliza lived near here, over in Riverside. She wrote to D.C. and requested a couple of Washington Navels, which she grew in her yard. They were a big hit, apparently. Soon, everyone in California was growing navels."

"Wow." I love stories like this. If Eliza Tibbets had been a ballplayer, she would have been an overlooked late-round draft pick out of nowhere who developed into an all-star. "Well done, Eliza."

Leslie nods. "She was also a suffragist, an abolitionist, and a spiritualist."

"Like, she conducted seances?"

"Exactly." Leslie chuckles. "A pretty remarkable woman."

I smile at her. "You're pretty remarkable, yourself."

Leslie's cheeks bloom a lovely shade of pink. "You know," she says. "I had a crush on you, way back when, before you moved away."

The semi-peeled orange remains cupped in my palm. My other hand smooths the pink of Leslie's cheek. "Well, now I've got a crush on you."

She reaches out, grabs a fistful of my shirt, and her lips find mine. The orange fumbles from my grasp.

I WAKE FROM THE LABYRINTH of orange trees, the illusory world of dreams, trailed by the words Eduardo's imparted to me. *Doug*, he said, his urgent eyes on mine. Though he had my full attention, he grabbed my shoulders, which were the bony shoulders of my adolescent self. *Doug!* Then, in his dream voice, which came out halting and robotic, he repeated to me three times:

Estamos girando. Regresando. La tierra. Yo a ti a ellos. El camino, la tierra. Valle blanco. Lejos de allá y de aquí. Regresa a ellos. Yo.

I fumble on my nightstand for my phone, the Spanish syllables echoing quietly on my tongue. I always wonder how much I'm remembering and how much my waking mind is fabricating. But aren't these messages only fabrications of my subconscious, anyway? Or do I truly believe Eduardo is speaking to me from another plane? It's a question I can't honestly answer.

Leslie lies beside me, still sleeping, I think, though I haven't yet learned the rhythms of her breaths, the coded messages of her murmurs and shifts. This is the third night we've spent together since our first kiss, a week ago. Clumsy and gentle sex. My body is in a perpetual state of dilated capillaries and sizzling nerves. Anxiety and joy are nearly indistinguishable in my mind.

I rise quietly, pull on my boxers.

Griffey stretches up from her spot at the foot of the bed and follows me down the hall. In the living room, I pause long enough to tap Eduardo's latest message into my phone.

My dog and I walk through the kitchen and out the side door. Together, we trudge to the edge of the gully and pee into the dark green bed of ivy that slopes down to the barely trickling creek below.

Then I work on translating the dream message. For certain words and phrases, I investigate alternatives, lists of synonyms. Eventually, I arrive at:

We are turning. Returning. The earth. Me to you to them. The road, the dirt. White valley. Far from there and here. Return to them. Me.

I try to sort out the meaning, and a tight breath rises in my chest. A pinch in my sinuses that feels like loneliness. Eduardo wants to go back. But to where?

Before I'm conscious of what my fingers are doing, my phone is dialing Mom's number.

"Well, good morning," she says, uncertainty evident in the lilt of her voice. "Where are you?"

"The farmhouse." I hope this answer will land softer on her ears than if I'd referred to it as *Dad's house* or *the house we fled*. "Remember, Mom? I moved—"

"Hmph. Of course I remember. I just thought, I don't know, you'd come to your senses." She sighs, and her tone lightens. "Or that maybe you'd come to Denver to visit your dear old Mom."

"I will. Once I'm settled. Maybe we'll drive out there."
"We?"

"Me and Griffey." Which is truly the most likely scenario, and yet it's Leslie I'm picturing in the passenger seat of Dad's old Buick. Since rescuing the car from the tow yard, I've cleaned the synthetic leather upholstery twice and have aired it out continuously. The reek of Marlboros is fainter now, but persistent. Maybe that residual stench is the form my father's spirit has taken. And it's up to me to exorcise his clinging grip from everything he once possessed and has now passed down to me.

"Your dog," Mom says. "Of course." A brief pause, a click of the tongue. "You know, I still think of Sergeant from time to time. He was a great dog, wasn't he?"

My beloved childhood pet, Sergeant was a magnificent German Shepherd, regal and broad-chested with a fine dark snout. That dog watched over my many adventures: climbing oak trees, scaling boulders, roaming the neighborhood with friends, bushwhacking across the seemingly infinite countryside. Sergeant kept track of Melissa and me when no adults were around—which was often. When I try to speak again, my throat is sticky with memories. "Yeah, Mom. He sure was."

"It's a shame he died so young."

Just eight years old. We got Sergeant as a puppy when I was four and my sister, two. He'd developed hip dysplasia, had more and more trouble getting around. There was never any talk of surgery, though I wouldn't have realized that was an option back then. When Sergeant vanished one day, Mom told us kids that he'd made the dignified choice to go off on his own and find a place to die peacefully in his sleep, or some crap like that. But I've always suspected Dad had put Sergeant down. I'd heard a gunshot the night before. Granted, that wasn't a rare occurrence in Orange Valley circa 1980, and especially not on our property, where Dad often hunted for rabbits and quail. Still, that connection had cemented itself in my mind.

"So," Mom says. "You're doing okay there? It's not too … I don't know. I have lots of mixed feelings about that place, even still. It seemed like paradise when we moved out there. It happened so slowly, everything going to hell."

"I know, Mom. I have mixed feelings, too."

I hear the living room screen door bap shut. As I walk around the corner of the house, the ground feels good and rough on the soles of my feet. The tangy-bitter scent of the lemon tree makes itself known to me. In the glare of sunlight cascading from the east, I watch Leslie settle into a battered Adirondack on the pink flagstone patio. Her strong, smooth legs unfold from beneath the hem of one my light blue dress shirts. I smile, point to the phone at my ear, mouth the word *Mom*. She nods, raises a mug of coffee. Not wanting to spoil her quietude, I turn and saunter away.

"But, hey, Mom. The reason I called, actually, is … do you remember Eduardo Ayala?"

"Oh, Eduardo." The tone of her voice is dreamy. I can picture the warm smile that accompanies her tone, but it's her face from decades ago that invades my mind.

What I saw at ten years old confused me. I'd gone out on my own, exploring the wilderness at the far edge of our property, snaking through the olive-green bushes and scrub. At the sound of a woman's sigh, I softened my footsteps, ducked low. Through the underbrush, I saw my mother in a yellow summer dress, palms planted against a twisty oak, her back arched, eyes closed, and that easy smile on her face. Eduardo stood close behind her, head tilted back as if to soak the sun into his handsome face. From that angle, they appeared fully clothed, but I had the queasy feeling that something intimate and illicit was nonetheless transpiring between their bodies. It's not a memory I've wanted to preserve, much less interrogate. And I sure as hell don't want those images circulating right now, while talking to my mother on the phone.

"Yes," she says. "I always liked Eduardo. I wish I knew … well, I was sorry when he left."

Left? Is that what she believes, or is she covering for her dead ex-husband? Or trying to spare me from the darkest depths of my father's nature? "Any idea where he came from? Somewhere in Mexico, right?"

When I turn around again, Leslie is staring at me, squinting through the morning brightness. I can't read her expression, can't begin to guess her thoughts. This realization—that we are mysterious and new to one another—sends a little shiver down the back of my neck, a pleasurable fear.

I've told her about my Eduardo dreams and how I've come to believe that he died before Immigration got their hands on him, that maybe he never made it back to Mexico. What I haven't voiced is my suspicion about exactly what role my father played in Eduardo's fate. Maybe her own father, too.

"Hmm," Mom says. "Somewhere in Sonora, I think. I remember looking it up on a map once."

I've been looking at maps, myself. The state of Sonora borders Arizona to the north, the Gulf of California to the west, Chihuahua to the east. From here, Sonora is a day's drive away—the day short or long, depending. I'm already projecting myself on the road, though I have no idea where I'd be going. "You don't remember the town, though?"

"No," Mom says. "Why do you ask?"

"I've just always wondered about him, that's all. About what happened to Eduardo, you know?"

"Mm." Mom grunts the syllable, as if she'd just stubbed her toe. "Yes. Me, too."

The line goes quiet while I wait for her to elaborate. I watch Leslie rise from the Adirondack and stroll my way. Backlit by the sun, her silhouette bleeds a lovely shape through the draped cotton of my sky-blue shirt. Her curious half-smile is a puzzle I want to solve. Thoughts of Eduardo and the fucked-up past shift toward the back of my mind.

"Well, okay. Thanks, Mom. I'll call again soon."

DAYS LATER, I FIND MYSELF standing before the diorama that dominates my childhood bedroom. Disbelief runs like an electrical current through the hairs on my arms. That figurine of the Vietnamese villager woman, I'd swear she wasn't kneeling before. Her hands are raised, head bowed in supplication. The hem of her pewter dress is bunched on the soil outside her thatch-roof home. A US Army private stands in front of her, rifle aimed at her skull. The private appears inanimate, just like a figurine should. But the villager woman? I can almost sense the caged-up energy in her terrified muscles, as if, despite her impulse to run from danger, she's trying to remain perfectly still.

Then a movement draws my eyes to a different home in this miniaturized tableau. The tawny bamboo walls, the front porch shaded by the overhang from the steepled roof. I stoop and crane my head, peer through the open doorway. A woman in a simple dress lies on a pallet on the dirt floor. A different US soldier stands in the foreground, his back to her, and gazes out the same doorway I'm looking through. His face is small, his features imprecise. My heart clunks in my chest because I'm sure of it: that's my father staring back at me.

I get the hell out of that room, fling the door shut behind me. Short, shallow breaths huff out of me. Already, whatever I just witnessed in the diorama feels like a fever dream, a spectral visitation.

I stumble into Melissa's old room, hoping to smudge away the afterimage of my father—not the figurine, but the actual soldier, the steely uniformed man I've seen in photos—standing in a shack in Vietnam. I try to focus, instead, on my transformation of this other room.

I've started cleaning out Dad's piles of hoarded crap, recycling what I can, trashing the rest in weekly batches. Every square foot I clear, I refill with baseball memorabilia. All the stuff Sheila once relegated to the garage. Of course, it's treasure in my eyes, and I'm giving every item its deserved placement: antique playing cards encased in

Lucite, autographed baseballs on stands, jerseys and pennants framed and hung on the wall. Some objects are tied to specific memories of players I've met or entire seasons I've covered for the paper. Others simply codify my love for the game. It calms me, being among these reminders of a sport that pulses like a vital organ within me.

Now better able to resume my day, I step outside into the clean heat of late June. The scent of eucalyptus purifies the air. I aim myself toward the garden, which is where I was headed before my hand reached out and opened that goddamned door.

Griffey, panting happily at my side, joins my walk around the perimeter of the former vegetable garden. The rectangular plot looks barren, just baked dirt and virulent weeds. Mom would be sick to see her once bountiful haven in such a state. In my very favorite photo of her, she looks to be dancing out from between two emerald stalks of corn, one arm thrown open, the opposite leg kicked back, and a rare goofy grin on her face. It's that spirit I want to revive here. In town yesterday, I bought several bags of rich soil, some packets of seeds. I'll see how much of Mom's heart I can channel back into the land. How much of Dad's neglect I'm able to disinter.

The short white picket fence surrounding the garden hasn't fared much better over the years. Peeling paint, leaning in places, and one section toppled over. But even I can mend a fence.

In the garage, I survey Dad's tools. They hang from arrays of hooks, rest in well-marked metal drawers, stand aligned in the corner, and sit neatly on the workbench Dad installed himself. The tools are plentiful in number and, unlike any other aspect of his existence, well-maintained. I imagine him standing in the exact spot my sneakers now occupy, his weathered hands organizing all these Phillips-head screwdrivers by length. And then electing not to bother with carrying a screwdriver back to the kitchen to tighten the pull on the pantry door. Instead, he would've wandered to the liquor cabinet. I picture him, highball in hand, bent over his creepy Vietnam diorama, like some reckless god of war.

Returning from her survey of the garage, Griffey bumps past my knees, wresting me from the bonds of speculation.

I grab a handful of nails, a hammer. On a nearby shelf, I find a can of white paint, give it a shake. All dried up. I'll have to make a trip to the hardware store. The brushes, however, are in fine shape. Of course they are. Dad always admonished me to clean them thoroughly after every use. A bath of warm water and dish soap in the utility sink, there in the corner.

The very same sink my father used on that long-ago night. What was he doing in here at that hour? What stains was he working to remove?

Chapter 4

1982

A sharp, percussive noise startled me awake. The clank-ing of metal on metal, as I would later surmise. The glow-in-the-dark hands on my nightstand clock read 3:10. Sweating in the summer heat, I peeled back the single sheet that covered me and went to the window. Movement drew my eyes to the flat, grassy field across the gulley. That's where I saw the image that would splinter into my mind and remain lodged there for the next forty years: a flashlight's beam and the black shape of a man against the bruised-purple sky.

I stood watching. From the man's rhythmic hunching and straightening, I felt certain he was digging a hole. Or filling a hole he'd previously excavated. On that moonless night, and from so far away, how could I be sure that the man shoveling dirt was my father? I couldn't be. Except that I felt him in the sutures of my stretching bones.

I tried to talk myself into venturing out there. But Dad hated to be interrupted. My lungs locked up at the thought of his scowl, his thick finger jabbing at my face. I stayed pinned to the wall beside my bedroom window and watched my father dig. What was he unearthing? Or burying?

A while later, the field went dark, and Dad vanished. I squinted into the night, as if that might help me to see.

Soon I heard footsteps on the gravel path that ran behind our house. Fear grabbed at my ribs. What if he caught me watching? I ducked below the window. Huddled and still, I breathed evenly through my nostrils. *Crunch-crunch, crunch-crunch.* Dad's uneven gait. The sound grew louder as he passed, then quieter again.

I guessed where he was headed: the garage. If I snuck out to the living room, I might be able to glimpse his entry or a light going on. But fright triumphed over curiosity.

I sat on the edge of my bed and waited. Sleep tried to pull me back under, but I stretched my eyelids wide in resistance. Finally, I heard the screen door bump shut and the shushing of bare feet on thick carpet. Then the quiet closing of my parents' bedroom door.

I kept waiting. Stood and stretched, pinched my cheeks. I watched the clock, phosphorescent minutes ticking off with aching slowness. I mentally scrolled through the latest chart of baseball's top hitters from the Sunday paper, picturing the men's confident faces from the playing cards in my collection. By the time I got to Dodgers second baseman Steve Sax, Dad's snores were leaking into the hall. I grabbed the Disneyland pen light I used for reading comic books past my bedtime. Then I slipped out of the house, across the driveway, and into the garage.

Near total darkness. I clicked on the pen light. Its beam was borderline useless but wouldn't betray my snooping. And I had deep muscle memory of the space, from all the times Dad forced me into being his helper. Mostly, I would fetch things: screwdrivers, oil cans, measuring tapes, fresh cans of beer. I knew right where the shovel leaned. Squatting before it, I aimed my pen light at the metal spade. Its surface shone from a recent cleaning, a patina of moisture still evident. At the juncture where spade met wooden handle, I found a chunk of wet mud.

I remembered my father's vow to Tomas Prochazka. *I'll make sure he's good and gone.*

In my blood, I felt something like a hum or a buzz. It pulsed in my gut. My forehead went clammy and hot. I told myself he'd buried something else out there—a neighbor's cat he'd run over, or money he'd embezzled from his clients. But the image struck me hardest was of Eduardo Ayala, lying dead in a makeshift grave, a spray of dirt landing on his once dignified face.

I scrambled for the utility sink, draped my head over the rim. I thought for sure I'd throw up, but nothing came. I dragged my fingertips along the sink basin, felt the porcelain, damp and cool. A TV detective would search for blood, but the notion roiled my stomach again. Instead, I opened the tap and splashed the streaming water on my face. If Dad had left any evidence behind, I'd conspired to wash it down the drain.

I'D ONLY SLEPT for a couple of hours when the rough grinding of an engine woke me. Was a crop duster flying overhead? Was a motorcycle pulling up to the house? No, the sound came from the wrong direction. I staggered to the window. Across the gully, in thinnest morning light, Dad was riding his lawnmower across the field where I'd seen him digging. Now, perched on his silver machine, he cut long swathes through the tall grass.

Images from last night crashed through my head. Shadows in the field, the shovel freshly cleaned. Had my father really killed Eduardo? I hadn't heard a gunshot. Of course, that's not the only way to kill a man. The Army had instructed Dad in other methods. And I'd witnessed first-hand his skill with a Buck knife on freshly hunted deer.

I opened my bedroom door and, a moment later, Melissa burst from her room, blocking my way.

"Omigod!" My sister had a whisper like a hissing cat. "It's, like, six in the morning. Why is Dad *mowing*?"

I shrugged, too tired and tense to manage anything else.

Melissa rolled her eyes—which could have signaled any of a thousand possible dissatisfactions—then turned and stalked off down the hall.

I followed her to the dining room, where Mom sat in her pale pink kimono, hunched over a mug of coffee. She looked up at us and winced. The glaze of exhaustion muted her typically bright, hazel eyes.

"Sorry, kids. Your father woke up with a burning passion to start growing crops. Or something."

"But Mom!" Melissa sighed. "We already, like, have a garden?" Her upper lip sneered on the word *garden*, as if the concept equated in her mind to *pile of manure* or *last year's fashion*.

"I know, sweetie." Our mother then turned to watch Dad on his mower. She seemed hypnotized by the motor's harsh rumble and the yellow haze of cut grass billowing in his wake.

After a while, she stood, walked to the kitchen, and pulled items from the fridge. We were soon eating bacon and scrambled eggs while Dad traded his riding mower for a rototiller. Its engine, too, made a horrible racket.

Worse than the noise was the queasy sensation that threatened to upheave my breakfast. I watched the now-shorn yellow grass turn into loose, brown soil. On the next two passes, there was a spot he appeared to steer around. The grave, I realized. He was hiding the naked gravesite by upturning all the earth in its vicinity.

Chapter 5

2022

Leslie looks beautiful in a jade-green scoop-neck dress, her smoky-blonde hair done up in what I think might be called a chignon. Her smile warms me as I reach for the bottle of merlot across the table and top off her glass. Ripples in the deep burgundy wine catch glints of light from the horribly dated chandelier that hangs above us. Its yellowy aura sets an appropriate mood: the dinner I've cooked for us—steaks, baked potatoes, and roasted broccoli—was a weekly staple of my 1970s childhood.

Dad taught me how to properly grill a steak. He was very practical in many ways. Very hands-on. Back then, no one spoke of emotional "tools" that a person might apply to a psychological issue, so my father channeled his angst onto the physical world. Tools were his tools. Hammers and barbecue grills, shovels and guns.

"You've drifted away from me," Leslie says.

I look up from the lumps of potato I've been poking with my fork. At least I haven't sculpted them into a white valley.

Her curious expression awaits me. Her eyes are working to read my face, my mind.

Sheila, over the course of our marriage, grew tired of this one-sided labor. I don't want to make that same mistake again.

"There's a question I've been carrying around with me for forty years," I say.

Leslie nods, leans forward. She's all in. "What question?"

"What if Eduardo wasn't picked up by Immigration and didn't leave of his own accord? What if he never made it off this property?" Sitting with my back to the field, I feel its tug at the nape of my neck.

Leslie's deep brown eyes narrow as she takes this in. "So, he was what? Murdered?"

My mouth goes dry as dirt. I swallow hard, chase it with wine. "By my father," I manage.

She shakes her head—slowly, absently. Not to refute my claim, necessarily, I don't think. I wait. A moment later: "Why do you think…?"

I tell her what I saw. Dad digging in the middle of the night. The next morning, how he laid the field bare. How Eduardo vanished at that very same time.

Leslie stares over my shoulder, into the gloaming distance. Her eyebrows rise. "Holy shit," she whispers.

"This all happened just days after our parents got together to talk about Eduardo."

Now she focuses her gaze on me again. "Wait, do you think my folks had something to do with it?"

"I don't know. Probably not directly. But Tomas got the ball rolling. He poked at my dad's insecurities, got him riled. I've always wondered, does he know something, your dad?"

Leslie emits a dark chuckle. "If he ever knew anything, that slate has been wiped clean. I mean, you've seen him, Doug."

"Sure," I say. Wiped clean? Or stored deep in some cob-webbed corner of his mind? "And I could be completely wrong about everything. But, with these dreams I keep having about Eduardo, I'm convinced it's his ghost who's talking to me. I know that sounds crazy."

Leslie's smile returns. "Well, I'm kind of a science girl, myself. But I never like to rule out anything. All theories should be investigated." She shrugs. "What if there's some other explanation? Like, maybe Eduardo got run over by a truck here in town. Or got killed in a bar fight. Or maybe he just walked right of here and found a job picking fruit in the next town over, and eventually he made his way back to… what's the name of the town in your dreams?"

"Valle Blanco."

"Right, right." Leslie's nodding again, looking off to the side, thoughts flicking through her eyes. Then she trains them back on me. "What would you say to some good old-fashioned research?"

THE ORANGE VALLEY LIBRARY is even smaller than I remember—around the size of my living room. As a kid, I would come here to check out biographies of baseball stars and Hardy Boys novels. Now, Leslie and I are here to search through the archives.

We sit tucked together at a narrow desk in one of the cramped reading rooms. I take a break from scanning microfiche film and stretch my eyes. Leslie is hunched over an old atlas of Mexico. Its pages are yellowed, its spine coming unglued. Because half the index is missing, she's poring over each and every detailed map, hunting for Valle Blanco. Her hypothesis is that the *white valley* from Eduardo's cryptic dream-speak is a town name, rather than a description. I've tried to google it, but nothing definitive came up.

Watching Leslie scour the pages of maps, I smile. Could our shared obsessive tendencies be the first step to love? Yes or no, I'm petrified of the answer.

I return to the microfiche reader. With its boxy monitor and tan chassis, it looks like a personal computer from the '80s. As a young sportswriter with a deep love for baseball's history, I used to spend far too many hours on similar machines, clunking and whirring through the stories and statistics of yore. Now I have before me a stack of compact film reels: scans of the weekly *Orange Valley Tribune* from the summer of 1982. Though I don't actually expect to find an article on the disappearance of an undocumented farm worker—especially from that benighted era—maybe some tidbit will lead me in the right direction. I'm compelled to try.

The headlines from my tiny hometown's past are so quaint, they read almost as satire: *Ice Cream Parlor Gets New Awning, Local Dalmatian Takes Third at Silver Bay Dog Show, Mayor on the Mend Following Fall*. All the same, nostalgia gets the better of me. I remember that new awning, the red of a maraschino cherry. I was classmates with the kid whose dog took home that ribbon. And I recall the mayor having taken a tumble. Onward I search, through the obituaries and police blotters—so few deaths or arrests in our quiet town. No mentions of a Mexican laborer perishing in Orange Valley.

By the fourth microfiche reel, discouragement has my shoulders slumped. The words begin to lose meaning.

"Found it!"

Leslie's exclamation shakes me, as if from sleep. She's smiling at me like a kid who's won a prize at the fair. I lay my hand on her back, fingers fanned between her shoulder blades. "Valle Blanco?"

"Yep." She adjusts the reading glasses on her narrow nose. "Right about… " Her fingertip hovers for a moment, then she stabs the page. "Here."

"Well, goddamn." I shake my head, amazed to see those dream-words manifested in minuscule black lettering against the expanse of sand-hued terrain.

"Now, let's see." Leslie flips the pages back until she lands on a different map that shows all of Sonora, segmented into rectangles labeled with alphanumerics. Again, her finger marks the spot. "Valle Blanco is somewhere in here, in the northwest region of the state."

"Not so far away," I say.

She tilts her head at me, dark eyes studying my face over the rim of her readers. "No. I guess it isn't, but—"

Cartel violence. "Maybe not so safe for a gringo like myself?"

Her eyebrows warp, lips bunched tight. My response has clearly failed to reassure her. Probably because I haven't promised not to go.

LATE JUNE, just outside Palm Springs, and the afternoon air is crackling, parched. Blue sky blazes above. As I pump gas into Dad's Buick LeSabre, the sun carves its way into the back of my neck.

Despite all the driving today, I feel exhilarated. One baseball stadium down, one to go. I spent the morning at Petco Park. I met a few of the Padres and got some baseballs autographed for my collection. More important, I interviewed a young man in the analytics department about the statistical models on the all-but-lost art of bunting and how its use has been affected by the National League having incorporated the designated hitter this season. I got enough good material to whip out an essay for the website Ben designed for me. I've already attracted a couple of advertisers whose obnoxious "impressions" are helping to pay the bills. Including gas for the Buick.

Back on the road, mountain ranges line either side of the Coachella Valley. When I was a kid, we came out here a couple of times, rode the tram to the peak of San Jacinto. To a Southern Californian, the green pines and spring snow had seemed miraculous. Down here on the desert floor, the vegetation is sparse and gnarled, and the sand is drained of color. A white valley.

But not Valle Blanco. I haven't yet committed to crossing the border.

I follow the map on my phone toward Palm Springs Stadium. A semi-pro baseball team plays there, and I've been invited to attend afternoon practice by their manager, Horacio Ramirez—one of the subjects of my book. I've been writing *Bad Hops* in fits and starts. But at least it's progress. Hopefully, I'll get an interview out of Horacio. He and I know each other from when I reported on Mariners games.

A dozen years ago, Horacio was among the team's top prospects. I would drive down from Seattle to Tacoma to watch his Triple-A games. A five skills player, he could hit, play outfield, and steal bases with the best of them. In his youth in Sonora, he'd earned the nickname El Mago—The Magician—and it had stuck. After getting a mid-season call-up to join the Mariners, Horacio played just seventeen games in the Show before tearing his ACL, ending his season. Then a drunk driver T-boned his car and fractured his hip. Despite years of rehabbing, he never climbed back any higher than Double-A. Eventually, Horacio took up coaching. Those are the brushstrokes. I want to flesh out his story, to share it with the world.

I'm also hoping to get some additional information from Horacio. He happens to come from a small town in north-western Sonora—just like Eduardo.

My phone guides me into the heart of Palm Springs, down streets lined with its namesake trees. Red tile roofs, beige stucco, buildings that lie flat and low, like dozing cats.

As I pull into a parking spot in the stadium's lot, the sharp bark of a batted ball rings through the desert air. I head straight in through a gap in a low chain-link fence, my walk unimpeded by bleachers, walls, security guards—all the things that make even most minor league stadiums appear fortified and regal.

Horacio sits on a folding chair behind the first base line, a stoic expression on his narrow face as he tracks his young crew's scrimmage in the torturous heat. The midsection of his light gray jersey has filled out since the last time I saw him, several seasons ago, during the twilight of his playing days.

"El Mago," I call out, and Horacio turns to face me. A generous smile stretches his neat goatee as he stands to meet me.

"Hey-hey, Doug." Horacio claps his palm against mine. He still has a powerful grip—the kind that could turn an inside fastball into a line drive. "How you doing, man?"

The simple question baffles me. I'm dazed by uncertainty, on so many fronts. I smile and nod. "Thanks for letting me intrude," I say. "It's good to be around the game again."

"It's a beautiful sport, no? At any level." Horacio's thick shoulders rise and fall, a comfortable shrug.

We spend a few minutes trading highlights from our recent lives. He and his wife have two kids now, own a house in nearby La Quinta, love the desert weather. When I boast of Ben's job accomplishments, Horacio congratulates me. When I tell him about my divorce and the death of my father, he murmurs and frowns in genuine sympathy.

I work the conversation around to my book project and pitch him the rough idea: the ups and downs of his career and personal life, the expectations and the hidden rewards. "What do you think? Can I interview you?"

"Sure, yeah. I'd be honored." With a chuckle, Horacio wings out his arms. "I always say I'm an open book."

We shake hands again—maybe to seal the deal, or maybe because he's ready to get back to managing his team. I've noticed his distracted glances toward the field. But I can't let him get away just yet.

"Another thing I wanted to ask you. I'm considering a trip to Sonora," I say. "What town is it you're from again?"

"I grew up outside Caborca."

"Yeah, that's near where I'd be going."

"Why?" His face tightens. "You know someone around there?"

"Oh. Well." I sigh. The notion is daunting. Then again, so is the notion of doing nothing, of leaving Eduardo's spirit unmoored within my dreams. "Do you know of a town around there called Valle Blanco."

"Eh, maybe so? I think it's kind of a ghost town."

Of course it would be.

Beneath the brim of his cap, Horacio's eyebrows turn doubtful. "Here's the thing, Doug…" He sucks air through his teeth. "That whole area, it's not a great place to be right now."

So people keep telling me. "I'll be careful."

"Right, yeah." Horacio smiles, but it's a hesitant smile.

"Oh, before I forget. Will you sign a ball for me? I'm a collector. Never got the chance before."

Like cracking through a thin layer of ice, warmth and ease return to Horacio's face. He turns and gestures to a young player slouched in one of the foldout chairs. "Hey, toss me a ball, okay? A nice new one, for my friend here."

WHY AM I STANDING in this room again? My childhood sanctuary, obliterated by my father and replaced by his shrunken ode to war. Morning's thin light falls across a fake village of fake huts, fake broad-leaf foliage bordering a fake muddy stream, fake Vietnamese civilians, fake American soldiers. But what these tokens depict was once very real. Real violence, real terror.

My phone is still in my hand. I slept like shit last night, woke up with Eduardo's latest dream message pulsing in my head. I lumbered out of bed and translated the Spanish syllables into my notes app as I shuffled down the hall. The result is glowing on the screen:

The earth was turning. He returned me. Orange Valley. I am not returning. White Valley. The earth was. Home. Not home. I am not.

Eduardo in his denim work shirt, cornered in the labyrinth of citrus trees. Sun-blazing oranges hung like ornaments around his head. Only the upper half of his body rose aboveground. His lower half hidden behind walls of excavated dirt.

I squeeze my eyes shut, then stretch the lids back open. The diorama blurs for a moment before crystalizing again. It's different from last time, the tableau altered once more. Behind the array of huts, all the villagers are lined up, down on their knees, fingers interlocked behind their heads. Five of the American soldiers stand before them, rifles aimed at the chests of the Vietnamese citizens. Only one of the soldiers hasn't joined the group of executioners. My father. He's placed his body between his brothers-in-arms and the woman whose hut he'd previously shared.

How is this happening? Horror and confusion shiver through my muscles. I grip the edge of the table with both hands. The fate of Dad's fucked-up little world is subject to my will. I could flip his diorama into oblivion. And I want to end it, don't I? So why do my shaking hands refuse to act?

I let go, turn away. I stumble, and Griffey yelps. Shit, I've stepped on her paw. My heart stammers as I stoop to comfort her. But her sad brown eyes look away, and she slinks from the room.

"Griffey, sweetheart. I'm sorry." I follow her down the hall. In the living room, I drop into a catcher's crouch, hold out my palm. "Come here, girl."

Begrudgingly, my dog returns to me. After a minute of petting, I even get a lick on the chin.

In the dining room, I stare out the window, at the field across the gulley. The grass looks pale, lifeless. How can it be that, since returning home, I understand my world less and less? I should brew some coffee, fry an egg, sit and read the box scores from last night's ballgames. Instead, I remain at the window. The pulse of panic begins in my gut. Just a flutter, at first. Then it spreads, reverberant in my lungs, a buzzing numbness in my extremities.

I need answers. And there's only one living person who might retain them.

I pull on jeans and head over to the Prochazkas. Griffey trots after me as I cut across the wild chaparral on my land and enter the neighboring orange grove. Despite my unimpeded view down the even rows, I keep expecting to find myself at a sudden dead end, as in my dreams of Eduardo.

I knock on Leslie's front door. Blood pulses in my temples and I'm snatching at breaths. I must've walked faster than I realized.

"Well, hey there." Leslie pushes open the screen door, a lazy smile gracing her mouth. "Come in."

It's still a wonder to me that I've kissed that mouth, that I could kiss her again right now if I wanted to. And of course I want to. But not right now.

"You all right, Doug?"

I turn to face her. Apparently, I'd been gazing around the living room. Looking for Tomas, I suppose. A frown has dipped between Leslie's eyebrows.

"Sure, of course." My chuckle sounds like a dry cough. "Your dad home?"

Her face puckers. "What's going on?"

"I know you don't think he'll remember. But he's our last chance. To find out what really happened."

She shakes her head, sighs.

"What does it matter?" Her eyes plead with mine. "My dad, your dad—they wanted Eduardo gone, and they got rid of him. Why'd they want him gone? Did my parents really think he might molest me? Was my mom screwing the help? I don't know." She throws up her arms. "But the end result's the same."

"No, I know. You're right. Maybe that part doesn't matter." I say this because it's clearly what Leslie wants to hear. And she probably *is* right. "It's how they reached the end result. It's how Eduardo died. That's what's prickling me."

"You sound pretty damn sure he's dead." Her eyes narrow, head tilts. "I thought the reason you went digging through the obituaries was to figure that out. But you didn't find anything, remember?"

"Why all the noise out here?" Tomas and his gruff voice. He stands in the doorframe, between hallway and living room.

Leslie shudders, turns to face him.

Looking past his daughter, Tomas's eyes meet mine. "Oh, it's Nick."

"No, Dad." Leslie sighs. "This is—"

"Tomas!" I boom my voice, cutting her off. As I step toward her father, I'm focused on his aged face, its vertical creases like folds in a drawn curtain, dark eyes that are portals between points in time, the narrow, frightened lips that part. Even without glancing at Leslie, I can imagine the consternation on her face. I raise a hand as I pass. *Let me try this*, the gesture is meant to say. I position myself before Tomas, his older body hunched and frail next to mine.

"What is it, Nick? What's going on?"

"That night," I say. "What we did to Eduardo Ayala. You remember, don't you?"

"What we did? What do you mean? Eduardo, he's right out there…" Tomas's gaze lifts from mine, seems to cloud over as he stares out the window or through a wall or into the murky recesses of his own mind. "I saw him only just…"

"When!" I grab his arm, jostle him. "When was the last time you saw Eduardo alive?"

"Doug, cut it out!" Leslie claps one hand to my shoulder, another to my chest. She peels me away.

I feel a sick twist between my ribs. My father's cruelty. I've let it sneak inside me.

No, that's not right. I asked it into my heart.

"Who are you?" Tomas's voice is quavering, his frail frame trembling. His wide eyes blink at Leslie. "Who is this man?"

She stares at me through a mask of scorn. I step back, and the corner of the coffee table jabs into my calf. "Sorry," I say. "I'm so sorry."

But my own words fail to drown out Tomas's, clanging in my head. *Who is this man?*

I'm not sure I know.

Chapter 6

1982

Out my bedroom window, the sun dipped into the cradle formed by branches of a magisterial oak. Early evening, the cocktail hour. Weeks had passed, and no sign of Eduardo. My parents fought more and more, about everything and nothing, fighting for the sake of fighting, it seemed, like boxers to the bell. Eduardo's name was no longer a subject of their arguments, the Prochazkas rarely mentioned. And yet, whatever had happened among them ran as an undercurrent of tension through my parents' voices.

I'd gone to Eduardo's trailer, in the clearing among the eucalyptus trees. This had been a few days after he disappeared—the first opportunity I'd had when both Mom and Dad were away from the house. My pulse had banged in my temples as I knocked on the little white trailer's aluminum door. When no one answered, I stepped inside. Dad had bought the junky thing at a police auction, on a whim. Soon after, Eduardo showed up on our land looking for work and had moved in. Very few traces of him remained: rumpled linens, cans of pork and beans in a cabinet, half a package of molding tortillas in the mini-fridge, blue jeans, denim work shirt, socks, underwear. But not his sturdy work boots. Nor his leather belt with its magnificent brass buckle.

Now, while the harsh words of another fight filled the house, I stepped into my sister's room. I held the shovel in my hands.

Melissa sat cross-legged on her bed, scrawling in a diary spread across the lap of her teal Dolphin shorts. With a sigh, she stopped writing and looked up. She frowned at the presence of a dirt-encrusted tool in her oasis of pastel colors and flower prints, where an Air Supply song poured like syrup through the air. "What."

"I'm going out to the field Dad plowed up. Come with me, okay?"

Her frown tightened. "Why."

"I think there's something he, you know, buried out there."

Her face softened, one eye half-closing in an expression of contemplation I recognized.

"In the middle of the night," I continued. "I saw him." I shifted back toward the hallway, hoping my body language would exert some magnetic force on my little sister. "Then he tilled up the soil to cover his tracks."

Melissa pulled out the small brass key that hung around her neck, locked her diary, and placed the rainbow-covered book in the drawer of her white wicker nightstand. She slipped her feet into old sneakers and pushed open the window over her bed. Within seconds, she'd popped loose the screen. This had also been my plan for getting out of the house undetected, only I'd pictured myself leading our escape out of my own bedroom window. "We better hurry," Melissa whispered. "Come on!"

She vaulted herself easily to the ground outside. I handed the shovel down to her, then craned my own gawky limbs up and over the windowsill, my shoes landing with a thud on the gravel path.

The setting sun was bleeding out across our property, molten colors on dry vegetation. Melissa and I jogged along the rear of the house, ducking below windows. The growls of our arguing parents flicked like embers out into the tinderbox air.

We crossed the wooden bridge. Above the chicken coop that housed our two remaining hens, a full moon made its first, faint impression against the lilac sky.

"This way," I said, turning to the field of turned-over soil and shoots of yellow grass, which had started growing back, like the stubble on Dad's face. The nearer we came to the vicinity of where I'd spotted him wielding the same shovel now in my hands, the less certain I felt about my ability to find the right location. The memory had seemed so clear in my head. But, up close, I couldn't trace the proper angle. I paused to look back at my bedroom window. My father might have stood right here. Or a dozen feet that way, or maybe even farther over in that direction.

"Is this it?"

Melissa's voice startled me, a jump in the throat. I walked over to where she was pointing. Sure enough, the ground there appeared to be slightly mounded. A coincidence? Possibly. The ground around here was far from level. But the dimensions looked about right for a grave.

"I think so." Hoping to fight off my nerves, I raised the corners of my lips, lightened my voice. "Nice job, Nancy Drew."

A wide, earnest grin spread across Melissa's face. Her childhood smile. It seemed like ages since she'd last shown me such an unguarded look. Then, as her eyes scanned the ground, I could see her measuring the gently sloping area. Her smile flagged. "What do you think he buried, anyway?"

My heart clomped against my ribs, a drumbeat I was certain my sister could hear. But her expression had gone neutral, betraying nothing.

"I don't know." I drove the spade into the earth—barely, but it was the gesture that mattered. "But I guess we'll find out."

The ground was dry, compacted. I was a wiry weakling, my efforts at shoveling pathetic. With each stomp and toss of the spade, I flung aside mere tablespoons of dirt.

Melissa took to pacing, sighing louder with each pass. Finally, she threw up her arms. "This is so lame. Why am I even out here?"

"Because … I think Dad might have …" I didn't know how to continue. Accuse him of murder? The idea of speaking the words seemed insane.

"Hey!"

His voice. Melissa and I turned as one. The shovel fell from my hands.

He'd just crossed the bridge, came running toward us. His stiff, wounded leg caused his torso to rock and lurch. He was carrying something. A long-handled tool? Fireplace poker? Through the encroaching twilight, I couldn't make it out at first. When I recognized Dad's hunting rifle, I raised my hands, like a criminal.

Melissa gently lowered one of my arms, and the other followed. "It's just Dad," she said, but her voice sounded unusually timid.

Our father's pace slowed to a brisk walk, and he lowered the rifle to his side. He stopped a foot away from me, looming in his military ramrod way, chest heaving and chin jutting like a blade. A wave of angry whiskey breath hit me, and all sensation left my body.

"What the fuck d'you kids think you're doing out here?" His eyes flicked from mine to Melissa's, then back again.

"Just messing around," I mumbled to the ground.

"Hey, be a man! Look me in the eye when you're lying to me." Dad's thumb hooked under my chin, raised my head with a jolt.

I heard Melissa's quiet gasp, sensed her sideways fade.

Our father had never struck either of us. Though many indiscretions were tolerated in our household, violence against family members was not among them. Dad exorcised his rage on coveys of quail, on darting jackrabbits, on aluminum beer cans balanced on the stumps of fallen trees. And possibly other targets.

"Nick!"

Now Mom was the one running toward us, the skirt of her sundress whipping at her knees. Dad's hand retreated from my face, and relief shook through my chest.

"My god." Mom was panting, palm pressed to her heart. She gaped at our father, a frantic intensity to her eyes I'd never witnessed before. "Were you planning to … to shoot our children?"

A mean grin cut across Dad's face. He coughed out a single laugh, as if the situation warranted nothing more. "Jesus, Maria. When I grabbed my rifle, I didn't know who the hell was out here, now did I?"

Mom flung out her arms. "Why would you need to shoot anyone, Nick?"

"The crops." Dad's shoulders drooped, his expression soured. "I thought someone was digging up the crops."

"What fucking crops?" Mom shook her head. "You mowed and you tilled, but you didn't plant a goddamn thing. Just forgot all about it. Like you forget about everything."

"No, no. That's not right. I'm sure … I must've …" Dad winced, looked away.

A hard silence fell. Time slipped into a lower gear.

As Mom's roving eyes took in the scene before her, I watched her expression slacken. The shovel on the ground, the scraped-up earth, the fear on Melissa's face, and whatever emotion my own gaze might have betrayed. I no longer knew what to feel.

"Nick." Mom's voice was barely audible, the syllable of her husband's name a bulge in her throat. "What have you done?"

"Nothing," Dad whispered. "Just what needed doing."

Chapter 7

2022

I'm driving the Buick at ninety miles an hour beneath a glaring Mexico sky. I bite into the first of two PB&Js I packed for the road. One for lunch, the other saved for dinner. Even with the AC streaming through the car, the wheat bread has turned to lukewarm mush. The peanut butter latches onto the roof of my mouth, and the grape jelly is sickly sweet on my tongue. I swallow the congealed mass and gulp water from my Nalgene bottle. The water's warm, too—all the ice melted hours ago, somewhere between Tijuana and the non-place that unwinds before me now. Gray-brown dirt, wisps of trees, olive-green creosote bushes, pale shocks of grass, and power lines that parallel the highway until they converge at the Earth's vanishing point.

How will I ever find a trace of Eduardo in all this emptiness?

According to the map on my phone, I'm nearing the blinking blue dot that marks my destination. But will I actually find Valle Blanco at that spot? The marker is just a guesstimate, based on the dog-eared and yellowing atlas of Sonora. When I zoomed in tight on the Google satellite image, there appeared to be a single rectangular structure just off the highway. Beyond the building, a dirt road or a dry riverbed, a pixelated nowhere.

Trying to stay awake, I tap on the steering wheel to the music playing. I found a CD wallet in the glove compartment and have already listened to the Allman Brothers, Tom Petty, and a mediocre Stones album from the '90s—which was probably the band's new release when Dad bought the Buick. Now I'm playing a scuffed Creedence compilation, John Fogerty singing about running through the jungle. I wonder what thoughts and memories tumbled through my father's mind whenever he listened to this song and its evocations of bloodshed in Vietnam. How much blood did he personally shed? What had killing meant to him?

I recently dug up his military discharge papers, trying to find some real-world connection to whatever's transpiring in the diorama he constructed. But there's no story to be gleaned from the sterile bits of information in his records. Neither commendations nor court-martials. He got drafted, got wounded, got out.

Sandwich finished, I toss the crumpled paper napkin to the floor mat on the passenger's side. I wish Leslie were sitting here beside me, but I couldn't have asked her to come along on this ill-advised trip. Besides, she's still pissed at me for interrogating her addled father. Or is she angry with me for leaving her behind? Or for putting myself in danger? Or because I foisted my dog into her care? Maybe all of the above. I haven't yet learned to decipher the registers of her various sighs.

Leslie did soften toward me before I left. I think she felt sorry for me after I told her about the last time I saw my father alive. This was twenty-six years ago, half my lifetime. I was newly married and had my first sports writing job, covering the Mariners' Triple-A club in Tacoma. But I knew I wouldn't feel like a real adult until I asserted myself against the man who'd raised me. I hadn't spoken to my father in seven years—not since a phone conversation during which he'd drunkenly called my mom a cold-hearted slut.

So, without phoning ahead, I flew down to San Diego, drove my first ever rental car out to Orange Valley, and surprised the bastard. It was the weekend. He stood in the driveway outside my childhood home, caressing a shammy cloth across the shiny new hood of this very same Buick. My father watched in silence as I emerged from the rental, an inscrutable squint in his eyes that inflamed my confrontational mood. I hadn't envisioned how any of it would go. Dad invited me inside for a drink. I told him no. Then I flat-out asked him, finally, whether he'd killed Eduardo. Dad started yelling: "How dare you accuse me!" and other meaningless bullshit. I yelled back, something about how he ruined my childhood. He catalogued all my faults. And Melissa's. And Mom's. And the many faults of every last person who'd ever crossed his path. I told him several times he could go fuck himself. That's pretty much all I remember from the verbal chaos of the thirty minutes I spent back home that afternoon. But I don't recall Dad ever stating, no, he did not in fact murder Eduardo and bury his body in a field in the middle of the night.

On my phone, the distance between the blue dot of my car and the other blue dot representing Valle Blanco has shrunk to almost nothing. If I were to drive another ten miles or so, I'd reach the town where Horacio was born, and that would mean I'd gone too far. A little farther still lies the city of Caborca, where a cartel recently killed several ordinary citizens. This bit of research on the area I decided not to share with Leslie, though I got the sense she already knew or at least suspected that such acts occurred here.

Up ahead, on the right… is that a road forking off the shoulder of the highway? As I ease off the gas pedal, I spot the sharp edges of a building, a slab of white against the beige horizon. I brake and steer hard into the turn. The Buick fishtails a little on the dusty road, racing my heart.

Taller de Autos, reads a sign on the building's façade. Car repair. From the shadows of an open garage, a man steps into bold daylight. A stocky guy, he's wearing blue jeans and a plain white tee. As I slow to a stop, he wipes his hands on a rag and greets me with a lift of his chin.

Stretching out of the car, I wave, offer a friendly smile. What should I say? How do I say it? A blankness pulsates in my head.

"Hola," I manage.

The man approaches, a wary pinch between his eyes as he glances at my car. He returns my greeting, asks how it's going. He speaks slowly, probably as unsure of my comprehension skills as I am.

But I can feel my brain engaging, switching from English to Spanish. I ask him whether this is Valle Blanco. He shakes his head, turns, and points somewhere beyond his garage, farther down the dirt road, which appears to quickly drop away.

Having clearly misjudged the satellite images of the area, I'd expected the eponymous valley to lie between hills that rise from the desert floor. Instead, it would appear the valley lies in an arroyo, below.

The mechanic looks to be around forty. Too young, I assume, to have known Eduardo. I ask him anyway—about Eduardo or anyone named Ayala from around here. No, sorry, not that he can recall. With each question I ask, the mechanic's eyes tighten one millimeter in apprehension. Fair enough. After all, I'm just some random gringo, interrogating him about the local population.

I smile and shake the man's hand, thank him effusively for his time. I ask him to please confirm that Valle Blanco can indeed be found in the direction I'm now pointing, partly because I'm nervous about driving off the edge of a cliff, and partly because I feel the need to seek his permission, as if the mechanic serves as gatekeeper for the land beyond his garage.

"Sí." He tilts his head to the west. "Por ahí."

I get in the car and pull onto the road. As I'm passing the garage, I glance over my shoulder. The moment before the man disappears back into the shadows, I see him lift a cell phone to his ear.

Pillows of dust rise around me, blocking the world in my rearview mirror. I tell myself he was simply calling a customer. Someone from the small town just down the highway. *Señora, your car is all tuned up and ready to go. Happy to be of service.*

When preparing for the trip, I talked myself out of bringing any of Dad's firearms. I was convinced the narcos would have known, somehow, and I would've ended up dead in a ditch. All I want is resolution. Why is that so much to ask for?

The dirt road slaloms, a gradual descent into the valley. Sure enough, the earth here looks bleached, or maybe ossified. Below, small houses dot the barren landscape. A river must have once flowed through here. Today, the land looks so dry, I can't imagine they get so much as a springtime stream.

The road levels out along the valley floor. I pass a small stucco house with a flat roof. No door, one window showing only jagged fangs of shattered glass. The next house, built of gray cinder blocks, looks similarly abandoned. As does the next, and the next.

At a small white church, I pull over and park. A bell tower rises proudly from the roof, despite the peeling paint on the walls and the unadorned, dirty windows. Next to the church is a modest cemetery: the reason I stopped. I get out and wander among weathered headstones and tilted crosses staked into the dry earth. The sun burrows into my skin, sucking it dry. If I were stranded out here, I wouldn't last a day. At the far end of the graveyard, I find the name AYALA engraved into a pair of headstones. A husband and wife, they died nearly a hundred years ago.

"Hola," calls out a voice behind me.

My heart plunges into my gut. I spin around, expecting a phantom.

A little old lady stands across the road, in front of a salmon-colored house—the only splash of color for miles around. Her platinum hair is pulled back in a plaited braid that drapes over the shoulder of her white dress and the delicate flowers embroidered there. Her eyes are on mine, but her expression doesn't betray any judgment about my presence. Does she receive regular visitations from strange white men? Or anyone at all? Maybe she's the mechanic's eccentric aunt or mother-in-law, and he checks in on her, supplies her with groceries and drinking water. Yes, I like this little story I'm constructing in my head. It calms the fluttering in my gut.

"Hola, señora." I smile and wave, the false cheer obvious to my own ears.

In response, the corners of the woman's lips rise slightly, adding new creases to the soft folds of her ruddy face. "Are you … how to say …?" She sweeps her hand through the air, across the unforgiving landscape, shakes her head.

"Perdido? No sé." I chuckle at myself, not knowing whether I'm lost. I walk toward her, a friendly amble. "¿Es este Valle Blanco?"

"Sí." She frowns, but it's a curious frown. An openness in her eyes, despite the thin gray fog of glaucoma.

I ask whether she knows the name Eduardo Ayala. I explain that he would have lived here some forty years ago, a young man at the time.

"Ayala, Ayala." She gives a hesitant nod. "Eh, sí." She explains that a family named Ayala lived here once and points in the direction of the house they occupied, but I can't make out which abandoned place she means, not that it matters. How long ago did the last Ayala leave? She shrugs, taps her temple, laughs. "Ah, memoria." Most everyone in Valle Blanco has left, she tells me. Gone to find work in Caborca, in Mexico City, in El Norte.

"Bien. Gracias." Defeat slouches my shoulders.

The old woman lays her hand on my forearm. The flesh of her palm is supple on my dry, hairy skin. She closes her eyes tight, chin lifted, as if she's looking toward the rim of the valley through the thin membrane of her rounded lids. I wait, very still, watching.

Her eyes reopen with slow flutters, like the wings of a waking moth. She nods, then turns and steps onto her shaded front porch. With a sweep of her arm, she beckons me to follow.

Though I'm of average height, I have to duck through the doorway. The air smells of earth and melted wax, and it's cool and dim inside the humble room. Concrete floor, white plaster walls, a kitchenette with ancient appliances, a futon couch covered by a wool blanket, a wooden table with two chairs. On a sideboard draped with gold cloth are ceramic statuettes of men and women in robes—saints, I guess—and an array of goblets filled with water. I'm totally unfamiliar with this manner of iconography, but even I know the figure hanging above the display: crucified Christ. Religion puts a squirmy feeling in my chest, but I want to be respectful, so I refrain from making any little noises of disparagement.

She offers me water to drink, which, apprehensive of local bacteria, I decline. She sits at the small table in the middle of the room and gestures for me to take the seat opposite. I plunk into the chair with a heavy sigh of relief, as if I'd been trekking for hours across the inhospitable terrain.

"¿Cómo se llama?" she asks.

"Doug," I say, hand on heart, as if pledging allegiance to my name. Mom named me after her father, a quiet and distant man, the opposite of the man she married. And divorced. The man whose surname—Lundvall—I continue to lug around. There's no winning, with names.

"Renata," she says, a subtle bow of the head.

She lights a trio of white candles. Her arms reach out across the table, palms raised. My host, it dawns on me, is a spiritualist. Like Eliza Tibbets, the horticulturist Leslie admires. My hands are trembling a little as I clasp Renata's.

I expect her to ask me questions or provide instructions. But Renata doesn't say a word. She simply shuts her eyes again. Am I supposed to follow suit? I hope not because my credulous mind won't let me. I need to watch for when her knee jostles the table or someone from the next room cues up a recording of spooky moans. Instead, all I witness is the side-to-side movement of her eyes beneath her lids, as if Renata has entered a dream state.

"Vaquero." *Cowboy*. Her lips have barely moved, and her voice makes only the faintest indentation in the air. Did she actually speak?

"Hm?"

"Sí. Un vaquero a caballo." As she goes on to describe the cowboy on horseback—the horse rearing up, the hat flying off—I see the object in my mind. The Spanish translation for belt buckle eludes me, so I stand halfway, say the words in English, and momentarily free one hand to point at the simple metal square that keeps my khakis from sliding down.

Renata's eyes open only long enough to confirm with a nod that, yes, this is the type of object she envisions. The cowboy belt buckle, she says, once belonged to Eduardo Ayala. "¿Verdad?"

"Yes." The word falls from me on a clipped breath as I drop back into my seat and clutch both her hands. "Sí, sí."

My throat's gone dry. I conjure an ounce of saliva, swallow it down. Now I want the water Renata offered earlier, but I wouldn't dare interrupt her.

A warm smile creases her face as she tells me, "Eduardo ha muerto, pero su espíritu está en paz."

Eduardo has died, but his spirit is at peace.

I exhale deeply. An odd mixture of sadness and calm swirl through me. Beyond calm: exhausted. My head droops and now my eyes do fall shut. I could fall asleep here in the dim quietude of the spiritualist's home.

"Pero tu padre." Renata clicks her tongue against her teeth—once, twice, three times.

By the third click, my eyes are wide open, heart stammering. I lean forward. "What about my father?"

She explains how Dad's spirit is not yet at rest. He's broken promises or left debts unpaid. She mentions a burial or maybe a grave, but I'm not sure whether she's referring to my father's body or a different body involving Dad. The old woman is murmuring, slipping into tangents. Or maybe she's delivering a perfectly articulated narrative, and I'm just too tired and rattled to keep up with her fluid Spanish. I should have been recording this on my phone. But I hadn't allowed the idea to form—it would have seemed a desecration to whip out such a device in front of all the watchful idols.

Renata falls silent. Gradually, her eyes drift open. Her gaze takes in my presence as if for the first time.

I force a smile, my face tight and edgy. My father's spirit, stranded between realms. Is that what I've just been told?

My host settles back into her chair, her expression neutral. Our session is over, I sense, our time together ending.

I stand, give an awkward little bow. "Gracias, Renata."

"De nada."

I take out my wallet. I brought three hundred dollars in cash. I extract two twenties and pass her the bills. She accepts them with many thanks. All the same, I worry I've cheapened the experience. I'm a clumsy interloper into her world. What the hell am I even doing here?

Despite my misgivings, I smile as I make to leave. Even as I bump the crown of my head on the low doorway, I keep smiling, reassuring the old woman that the pleasure was mine, that I've had a profound experience.

When I slide back into the Buick, the trapped heat envelopes me. Am I woozy from dehydration? From smacking my skull? Or is my wobbling mind an after-effect of the spiritualist's probing? I start the engine, crank the AC, and guzzle lukewarm water.

Back I go, climbing out of the arroyo and away from the empty town, with its paucity of answers. Eduardo's spirit is at rest: this much I've absorbed. I suppose that should be enough. But dissatisfaction burns like a rash on my skin. Dissatisfaction and shame. I care far less about the disposition of Eduardo's soul than I'd like to admit. This whole idiotic journey, it's really all about my father. Of course it is. Because I want to exonerate him? Or to prove his guilt?

Sunlight flashes on the road ahead, a reflection. Metal, glass. A dark blue sedan parked sideways across the narrow lane, near the mechanic's garage. The words *Policia Municipal* painted in white across the flank. Two officers in dark blue uniforms stand at either end of the car. Dark sunglasses, no hats. One of the cops—a guy with a mustache—steps forward, holds up a hand for me to stop.

Panic rattles through me. This is where I'll be shot dead, or held for ransom, or who knows what. I could veer around them, floor it through the countryside. There isn't much to distinguish the dirt road from the surrounding landscape— just a few gray-green bushes, the occasional cactus. But they'd only hunt me down, wouldn't they? Didn't some family of *turistas* recently try to escape such an ambush, only to be murdered moments later?

My foot finds the brake pedal. I throw the Buick into park and roll down the window.

Officer Mustache rests his hand on his sidearm as he approaches. From the silver in his sideburns, he looks to be around my age. His sidekick, a baby-faced guy, strolls along the passenger side, his blue belly moving past the windows like a sea creature in an aquarium. Mustache leans down, fixes me with his bug-eye sunglasses.

"Hola, señor," I say. Once again, I'm all smiles. *Playing innocent*, I think. No, wait: I am innocent. "¿Un problema?"

"Inspection," he says in English. Then he steps back two paces and draws his revolver. My breath chokes in my throat. But he doesn't aim the gun at me, just waves it lazily and tells me, "Out of the car."

My entire body is vibrating with fear. I fumble with the latch. The door feels immensely heavy, like a mountain of lead. My body is limp, muscles gone to slush, as I climb out of the car. Mustache points the barrel of his gun at the spot—a patch of dirt just a few feet from his side—where he wants to me to wait.

I stand there and watch Babyface circle the car, performing his so-called inspection. He climbs into the driver's seat. The Buick's engine continues to idle. It would be so easy for him to drive it away, for Mustache to blow my brains out. I see it all happening, as if from a great distance—from way beyond the mechanic's garage, all the way to that mesa over there, that flat and barren space that exists outside the governance of time, a place so removed from the world's concerns that not even a minor death could occur there.

"Five hundred dollars."

I turn to Officer Mustache, stare at the shiny black plastic where his eyes should be.

"Inspection fee," he says.

"Sí. Okay." The terms of a financial transaction. There's something comforting in the mundanity of this. Even as I fish out my wallet, knowing that the amount of cash it holds is roughly half of what's been requested, I start to feel myself again. Inhabited. Almost gleefully, I pull out the bills. We're going to barter, Officer Mustache and I. Right? Isn't this how it works in other countries? The initial price is always inflated, that's just part of the game, everyone knows it, everyone plays along.

The Buick's trunk pops open. Officer Babyface saunters back to have a look. He won't find anything in there but a spare tire, jumper cables, an emergency kit, a spare blanket tied up with a bungee cord.

"Two-sixty." I hold out the cash to Mustache. "Sorry, it's all I have."

He swipes it from my hand, counts the twenties in near-silent whispers. "Veinte, cuarenta, sesenta…" When he finishes, he folds the money into the pocket of his uniform trousers. He nods at me, apparently satisfied.

The pain in my abdomen registers in my brain an instant before I realize what's happened: the fucking cop—or is he a fake fucking cop, and does it really matter at this point?—has punched me in the stomach. I double over, a sickly moan coming out of me. Now I'm staring at his cheap black tennis shoes, wishing I could stop myself from moaning, wishing I could stand up straight and disprove how easily defeated I am, how flabby and weak. Wishing I weren't the helpless, stupid gringo that both Mustache and Babyface and, let's face it, their opportunistic amigo the mechanic, instantly knew me to be.

"Not enough money," Mustache says, as if his objection needed to be verbalized.

I manage to stretch myself back up to semi-standing, an old-man hunch. My flesh stings from the impact of the punch and I'm panting like a dog. I wish Griffey were here. No, I wish I were home, back in Orange Valley, with my dog and my maybe-girlfriend. I'll have to call Leslie, beg her to wire the remaining cash to the account of some thug in bum-fuck Mexico. I should have listened to her, should've listened to Horacio.

"Baseball," I find myself saying. "Do you like baseball?"

"Sí." A funny smile wrinkles Mustache's mustache. "Me gusta el béisbol."

The autographed baseballs from the San Diego Padres are still in my car. I'd meant to retrieve them any number of times, but had been consumed with writing my book and wrestling ghosts. I explain to Mustache, in a mixture of stammering Spanglish and pantomime, what I have to show him. Right there, I gesticulate for Officer Babyface. "Exactamente, en esa bolsa, behind the backseat. Sí, sí."

Babyface sets the cuboid padded bag on the hood of the car. He leans back, arms extended, and unzips it slowly, as if rattlesnakes might be coiled inside. Then his plump cheeks ripen into a smile. "Las pelotas de béisbol."

He carries the open bag over to us. I pluck out a ball, read the name inscribed on the white cowhide, between the red stitches. It's the name of a good player: a starter, but not a star. Just thinking about baseball is a balm to my nerves. I raise my eyebrows, eke out a hopeful smile.

Mustache frowns. "You have Juan Soto?"

The Padres signed Soto, a multi-million-dollar outfielder, at the trade deadline, just a couple of days after my visit to the workout room. No, I inform Mustache. Nor Manny Machado, nor Yu Darvish.

I shuffle through the half-dozen balls, but none of these autographs are from famous players. My eyes keep darting to the pistol dangling in Mustache's hand. Despite the heat, icy dread seeps into my veins. A clammy sweat sheens my forehead.

Then I see it. The signature of the local hero, the Sonoran whose talents should have made him a perennial Big League all-star. I hold up the ball by my fingertips. "¿Conoces a Horacio Ramírez?"

For the first time that afternoon, Officer Mustache's lips crack into an earnest grin. Even through his dark shades, I swear I can see a childish wonderment in his eyes. He plucks the ball from my hand, and his voice goes quiet, breathy with awe: "El Mago."

Chapter 8

1982

Mom woke me at dawn, the sunlight in my bedroom uncertain and pale. Per our mother's instructions, Melissa and I had packed the night before. Meanwhile our parents had fought—their final face-to-face confrontation. Now Mom's eyes looked heavy and dark, a twitch at one corner. She must have stayed up all night after Dad passed out. I'd been up late, too, terrified that my father would finagle a way to keep us here, prisoners in his palace of rage. I was also worried about moving to Denver, a city I'd only visited twice. Mom's reclusive brother, Uncle Robert, lived there. Serving in Vietnam had damaged his psyche, but in a way opposite to my father's. Uncle Robert was a quiet and defeated man, but a good guy. He'd agreed to put up his sister and her two tween kids.

I pulled on the shorts, shirt, and shoes I'd set out the night before. As I stepped from my room, all I heard was a horrible silence. Holy hell. Mom and Melissa, they'd left me behind, alone with Dad. I sucked in air but couldn't exhale. Then the clinking of a spoon unzipped my lungs. I hurried to the dining room, where my sister sat, bent over a bowl of cereal. Another bowl awaited me at my seat. A seat that would soon no longer be mine. I'd have to claim a different chair, in a different house, in a different city. In a month, we'd be attending a different school.

Mom strode in from the kitchen, turned around, took a step, blinked, turned again. She'd pulled her hair into a sloppy ponytail. She wore her gardening outfit of old bell-bottom jeans, worn-out tennis shoes, and a cotton shirt that had been laundered into a pale and shapeless thing. She gazed at me as if my entire body had suddenly rearranged itself into an unrecognizable form. "Doug, eat." She spoke in a whisper, pointing at the bowl of Frosted Flakes. "We need to…" Then she lifted a cardboard box from its barstool perch and carried it out the kitchen door.

As we shoveled cereal and slurped milk into our mouths, Melissa and I exchanged nervous looks. She hadn't been her usual blustery self since that awful night, a week earlier, when Dad came charging at us, rifle in hand.

"It'll be all right," I said.

"I know." The dismissive snip in her voice seemed like a good sign.

We set our bowls in the sink. Eventually, it occurred to me, Dad would have to place those bowls in the dishwasher. He could change the oil in a car and skin a rabbit, but did he even know where to put the soap in the dishwasher? The first pang of guilt hit me as I walked back to my bedroom to gather my possessions. We were abandoning my father.

In the driveway, Mom was shoving a suitcase into the way-back of the station wagon. I wedged my wooden orange crate of comic books into the haphazard heap of our belongings. Melissa loaded in her makeup bag, and, for the next ten minutes, we made a succession of trips back and forth, careful not to slam doors or stomp down the hall past where Dad remained unconscious.

I called dibs on the passenger seat. Melissa sat in the back, surrounded by piles of linens. Mom got behind the wheel and power-locked the doors.

Panic rushed through my head. We'd forgotten Sergeant! I nearly called out. Then I remembered: my dog had died a year ago. Died, or was put down.

I was buckling my seatbelt when Dad staggered out of the house. He loped across the driveway, barefoot in boxers and undershirt, hair mussed. He was squinting in a pained way, as if a squirt of lemon juice had gotten in his eyes. "Goddamnit, Maria!"

Mom's hand shook as she fit the key into the ignition. The engine rumbled to life just as Dad smacked the driver's side window. My heart stuttered. Melissa gasped. Mom yelped and shrank away.

"Okay, Jesus." Dad raised his hands, took a step back. He had a rare, wounded look in his eyes, but the pulsing vein at his temple revealed his well of anger. Though clenched teeth, he said, "Don't I get to say goodbye to my kids?"

"No!" Mom aimed a finger at him, like she did when she used to scold Sergeant for digging food out of the trash. "You gave up that right. You and your goddamn guns."

"Oh, come on! I've only ever protected us, provided for us."

Mom just shook her head. Then she jerked the shifter into drive and the station wagon lurched ahead. My stomach sank, like at the beginning of a roller coaster ride. Mom clutched the steering wheel as if she might otherwise fall off the face of the world.

"You bitch!" Dad yelled we passed. "You're gonna regret this!"

We all turned to watch as Dad started running, lopsided, after the car. His eyes were wide open now and glazed with animalistic determination. I really believed he might catch hold of the bumper, that his fury would obliterate us. Everything went strangely quiet.

Then Mom stomped the gas pedal, and our skidding tires hissed on the dirt drive. Dust plumed. Through the sungleaned particles, I watched our father stumble and topple to the earth. A second later, the driveway curved around the white picket fence that surrounded Mom's vegetable garden, and Dad disappeared from sight.

Chapter 9

2022

Downtown Orange Valley is a single block of businesses lining both sides of the main drag. The ice cream parlor is wedged into the middle, between a realtor's office and a pet store. The red awning that was newsworthy in 1982 has faded considerably. Inside, the place looks mostly the same as I remember it. I mention this to Leslie, who sits across from me.

"I'm not sure I can picture the difference between now and then," she says. The vinyl booth behind her was once the color of a maraschino cherry. Now it's pinkish and parched. "Except I do remember playing an Evel Knievel pinball machine here when I was a kid." She tilts her head toward the far wall, where a couple of newer video games now stand, looking forlorn. It's a weekday, early afternoon, and school's back in session now. The place is quiet.

"That's right." I can almost picture the graphic of Knievel on his motorcycle, riding through flames. I smile at our shared recollection.

Leslie's cheeks pucker as she sucks mint chip milkshake through a straw.

Scooping a bite of coffee ice cream from a waxed paper cup, I say, "When I was down in Mexico . . ."

Her nod is barely perceptible. Mostly it's the intensity of her deep brown eyes that tells me she's listening extra hard, that my tone of voice must have indicated a rawness in my heart, a divulgence on the way.

"And those cops were shaking me down," I continue, "there was a minute or so where I was really afraid. When that cop punched me in the gut and I looked down at the gun in his hand? I pictured myself dead in an arroyo. I thought of you, of wanting to get back to you. Well, and Griffey, too."

Leslie reaches across the Formica tabletop, wraps a strong orange-picker's hand around mine. Her eyes glisten in the sunlight that blazes through the plate glass window. She looks up, blinks wetly, looks back at me. Then a sly smile nudges onto her lips. "You're not about to propose to me, are you, Doug?"

"No." I exhale a small laugh. It feels good, as if the room just expanded after holding its breath. "But I am telling you that I love you. And I'm not going anywhere. Okay?"

I SWEEP THE METAL DETECTOR through the high, golden grass. I try to keep the coil just an inch off the ground, as the manual advises. With each arcing pass of the detector, the grass blades bend low, then spring back upright, seemingly indifferent to my presence. Or does this field harbor malicious intent? Is it trying to keep me from finding evidence of my father's crime? Or is Eduardo not actually lying dead and buried in the ground beneath my feet? Eduardo and his large brass belt buckle.

Maybe twenty yards away, Leslie stands in profile, the angle accentuating her face's slender, foxlike features. As she stoops to pick up the tennis ball that Griffey has dropped at her feet, the afternoon sun catches golden highlights in the waves of Leslie's silt-blonde hair. She fits the ball into the plastic flinger and sends it hurtling into the pale blue sky.

I watch Griffey bound after the ball—yellow lab in yellow grass. My dog keeps her eye on the prize as she runs, like a shortstop tracking down a weak pop fly in shallow left field. She dips low to retrieve and, for a moment, is invisible. Then her head pops above the grass, a slobbery green tennis ball in her smiling mouth. She circles around and gallops back toward Leslie. And the cycle continues.

As do my own cycles, both physical and emotional. I take another step forward, sweep the detector through the grass. Once again, the device's silence drains an ounce of happiness from my body. So I look again to Leslie and Griffey. One has forgiven my recent bouts of stupidity, and the other loves me unconditionally. Leslie's told me that she loves me, too. But her love comes with implicit conditions—a wariness that I sense. She's known my adult self only at my most fragile. A man prone to occasional acts of lunacy. I hope to gradually prove myself a stable and reliable person. For Leslie's sake, and for my own.

I step forward, sweep the detector right, then left. The device emits one of its little electronic squeals. The first hit I got, an hour ago, had me tingling with anticipation and dread. I'd grabbed my shovel—a newly purchased shovel, not my father's, which I'd donated. I'd dug up nothing but an empty hole.

I make a shorter sweep over the area, and the detector whoop-whoops, sounding like a slide trombone on helium. After marking the spot with a red poker chip I recently found beneath the kitchen stove, I retrieve my shovel. It'll probably just be a tarnished buffalo nickel, or one of Dad's old shell casings. I've pretty much convinced myself that either I hallucinated the entire vision of my father burying Eduardo or the bastard exhumed the body and reinterred the remains somewhere else entirely—a spot where the evidence would never be found.

But I can't stop myself now. I stomp the blade through the hard earth and stringy grass roots. Again, and again, and again. Is this a new act of lunacy? My forehead was already beading with sweat in the late summer sun, and now my whole upper body is drenched. I heave out a hunk of dirt. Nothing yet. I dig deeper. A few feet down, the shovel strikes something hard. Kneeling over the hole I've dug, I fish around with my fingers in the loose soil. A thin edge of metal. And some material, maybe leather. And the hard thing: not rock, but smooth bone.

"Leslie." I hear the shakiness in my voice. As I fling dirt from the hole, it feels like there's a drill bit spiraling into my chest. I know what I've found even before I've worked it free. It's not Eduardo or his belt buckle.

The leather dog collar disintegrates as I pull it from the ground. But the aluminum tag is intact, barely worn. I rub the dirt away with my thumb. Sergeant's name is stamped into metal in capital letters, followed by the seven digits of my childhood phone number. Dad's number, until a few months ago. A number I hadn't dialed in decades, but could never dispel from memory.

I'm half-aware of Leslie's shadow hovering over me. Half-aware of her hand caressing circles on my back. Half-aware of the tears that flood my face, the breaths that rattle out of me. The other half of me has fallen forty-two years into the past. A gunshot in the night. Sergeant taken from me.

Licks land on my chin, warm and wet, an urgency in the rhythm of Griffey's tongue. The past melts away, and my eyes focus on the living dog before me. The soulfulness and love in those brown eyes stare unguarded into my mine. I wrap my arms around her and hold on tight.

TILTING BACK MY HEAD, I drain the last warm swish of beer and plunk the bottle down on the dining room table. Four empties lined up now—a squadron of hollow soldiers standing at attention. Fearful of turning into my father, I've always kept an eye on my drinking. At the moment, I don't fucking care.

I stare out the window at the darkened field. The dry grass is unmoving beneath the pale light of a crescent moon. Could anything good ever be made of that swath of land?

Loneliness bristles in my chest. Leslie, having spent the afternoon and evening with me, left a while ago to relieve the healthcare worker and tend to her increasingly addled and faltering father.

I tug my phone out of my pocket, tap Melissa's name. My sister answers on the third ring.

"Doug? You okay?" Her voice is sticky with sleep.

I check the clock on the wall. Just after ten. An hour later in Denver, and she's an early riser. Shit.

"I'm okay. Well, no, I'm not."

"Why? What's wrong?" Though Melissa is whispering, her tone fizzes with urgency. I picture her fumbling out of bed, trying not to disturb her husband. Bare feet padding on loop pile carpet. Closing herself in the bathroom as she awaits my dire news: colon cancer, bankruptcy, her nephew in jail.

"It's all right. Sorry." A sob hiccups out of me. "I shouldn't have called so damn late."

Melissa sighs. "Just tell me what's going on, okay?"

"It's Sergeant."

"Honey, you're drunk. Sergeant's been dead for a long, long time."

"No, I know."

"You mean Griffey? Doug, is Griffey—?"

"She's fine, she's great. Let me start over." I lift one of the empty bottles to my lips. It is truly, completely empty. "Today, out in the field across the gully?"

"Yeah." The way my sister says this, on a tight exhale, I know she's picturing that twilit summer evening forty years ago. Dad and his shotgun.

"I dug up Sergeant's remains."

Over the cellular waves, a thousand miles between us, Melissa's quiet gasp crackles like static. "Jesus."

This afternoon, Leslie helped me to disinter the bones. They were arrayed just as my father had left the body, after he put a bullet through my dog's skull and then tossed him in a hole. Maybe that's not a fair assessment. Maybe he laid him gently in that hole? I don't know and I don't care. I never got to say goodbye. And there was no ceremony back then. So Leslie and I held a memorial for Sergeant today. We wrapped his remains in a quilt I found stashed away in the top of a bedroom closet—one of the items Mom forgot during her frantic attempt to get us packed into the station wagon—and we gave Sergeant a proper burial in a corner of the garden, where vegetables are sprouting once again. Leslie held my hand while I read a poem from Twain. *Warm summer sun, shine kindly here.*

"Dad killed him, you know." My voice is shaky on the phone. "Just took Sergeant out to the field and shot him in the head."

"I know," Melissa says, her voice soft and flat. "I mean, of course that's what he did. I'm really sorry. I'm sure it's what Dad thought was right." A throaty sound comes through the phone, one of my sister's ironic laughs. "But, shit. That doesn't make it better. I just … I know how much you loved that dog."

"Yeah." Now it's my voice that comes out hushed.

"Doug? Are you sure it's such a good idea, you living there? With all those ghosts?"

I sigh. "No, I'm not sure." Then I think of Leslie, just an orange's throw away. Not much farther than the center field wall to home plate. "But I think it could be. I think, maybe, I can make it good."

IT'S PAST MIDNIGHT, and those four beers still have my brain feeling muzzy. I push open the door to my former bedroom, and the stagnant air pushes back. I haven't set foot in here in weeks. I shut the door behind me, to keep Griffey away.

Another thing that got left behind, all those years ago: an aluminum baseball bat. It's short, just 29 inches, one I'd outgrown a couple of seasons before we moved. Now, in my adult hands, it weighs almost nothing. Easy to swing, and swing hard.

The way Dad's diorama stands there, consuming the better part of the room, strikes me as confrontational, almost smug. I raise the bat, tighten my grip. Loosen, tighten. Loosen, tighten. Test the balance, choke up a little higher on the handle for better control.

As I step up to the edge of the diorama, I can tell right away that something has changed in the Vietnamese village. I feel it before I see it, as if the visceral jungle air is communicating through the hairs on my arms, the muscles at the hinges of my jaw.

The pewter soldier—the one who is unmistakably my father—has moved yet again. He's no longer standing before any firing line. Now, behind the row of simple homes, the bodies of villagers lie dead on the ground, dabs of blood painted on their chests and heads. The American soldiers are huddled back on the far side of the village, where they first emerged. But my father's not among them.

I lower the bat, let it fall to the carpet below. Stooping down, I peer into the hut where I'd found Dad the time before. He's not there. Nor is the local woman I'd seen lying on the pallet.

When I stand up straight again, the Vietnamese village shudders and blurs. I place my palms on the fake grass at the edge of the diorama. With deep breaths, I gradually steady myself.

My eyes sting from staring so intently at this awful scene. My dead father's replica of a faraway place and time. A single day, perhaps. Or only a handful of minutes. And yet, whatever transpired in that village apparently haunted him for half a century. Or did it fill him with nostalgia?

I can't imagine either. The absurdity of it all makes me giggle. And, for the second time in less than twenty-four hours, tears stream from my eyes. That's one for the record books. If only Sheila could see me now. My ex-wife would be astonished at the display of emotions. I swipe the wetness from my eyes.

Now I see him. The figurine of my father dressed in Army camouflage, a white bandage wrapped around his thigh. He's at the opposite edge of the diorama from his brothers in arms. Despite the injury, he appears to be walking into the jungle, a dense wall of trees and broad-leaf foliage. He's carrying the woman from the hut. Is she dead? Is he searching for a burial spot? No, looking closer, I notice her arms are wrapped around his neck. And she looks up at him, her eyes wide and bright— with terror or with love?

I stand here for a while, taking this in. Is this Dad's fantasy of what *should have* occurred that day in Vietnam? Or is this an awful portrayal of what actually happened? What he perpetrated?

Either way, I'll never know.

I think of Renata, the old spiritualist from Valle Blanco. She told me: *Tu padre, no ha encontrado la paz.* Do I want him to find peace? Maybe, through observing the diorama, I've accidentally helped him to move on. Or this room really is fucking haunted. I decide to be okay with the not knowing. Or, at least, to try to be okay.

Chapter 10

2023

From the bed of Leslie's pickup truck, I grab a lime tree sapling in a plastic pot and head across the white wooden bridge, Griffey trotting along behind me. We've already made several such trips today. In the gully below, the muddy stream rushes between ivy-coated banks. The sapling is maybe two feet tall, just a thin gray stalk with green leaves poking up from the dark, rich soil. Some of that soil has smudged the front of my flannel shirt—long-sleeved, due to the coolish February air. But winter here in Southern California is nothing compared to the many seasons of wet, cold, and gray I endured in Tacoma and Seattle.

Looking beyond the dilapidated former chicken coop, I marvel once more at the large expanse of freshly turned dirt. I managed to tune up Dad's old rototiller and bust up the earth out here, just as I once watched him do. But, whereas Dad failed to follow through—*you didn't plant a goddamn thing*—I'm starting a small citrus orchard. With Leslie's help, of course.

She's crouched at the far end of the field, yanking up stray roots from the evenly spaced holes I've dug. As a complement to her orange grove, we're planting lemon, lime, and grapefruit trees on my property. Eventually, maybe there'll be enough yield for a booth at the Orange Valley farmers' market. In the meantime, the physical activity is good for me.

Over the last six months, I've spent too many hours at my computer, writing about baseball. My blog pays the bills and requires fresh content. As much as I enjoy drumming up news and opinions for the website, my passion project is *Bad Hops*. Having met up with Horacio a few times during the off-season, I'm feeling good about the chapter devoted to his life, both in and out of baseball. Enough time has passed that I'm now glad I drove to Sonora, to the area where he's from. Though the trip to Valle Blanco did nothing to help me understand the disappearance of Eduardo Ayala, my having experienced both the region's desolate beauty and threat of violence has informed my biography of Horacio. Or so I tell myself. If I had the spare cash, I'd also travel to Venezuela, the Dominican Republic, the American Midwest, and elsewhere, in order to witness where my other subjects were born and raised. In the cases of some historical figures, I'd also need a time machine. Even without hands-on research, my book is coming along well. I've sent a proposal to several agents. Planting baby citrus trees helps take my mind off waiting for their replies.

Of course, the greatest beneficiary is my soul, if such a thing exists. Transforming the land my father neglected: could the act be more plainly symbolic?

I squat next to Leslie, watch her tug out a stubborn root. I set the pot on the ground.

"Got that son of a bitch." With a laugh, she tosses the root aside and blots her sweaty forehead with the back of her wrist.

I smile, glad to see lightness returning to her eyes. Tomas passed away back in November, and Leslie has spent these last few months wrestling with the complexities of grief. She feels relieved, she's told me, that she no longer has to care for her addled and difficult father. But her relief is coiled with a great sadness that she was never able to crack his emotional shell, and now she never will.

About my own father, I'm less conflicted. I never could have hoped to change him. And, even if he were still alive, he'd never reveal what happened on that night, over forty years ago.

Neither will Eduardo, nor his once restless ghost. Renata's words return to me: *Eduardo has died, but his spirit is at peace.* I believe her. He hasn't visited my dreams for months. Shortly after Leslie and I reburied Sergeant's remains, we erected a separate memorial to Eduardo: a white cross in the eucalyptus clearing where his trailer once stood.

In another attempt to clear away the past, I dealt with the diorama. Having nearly laid to waste the Vietnamese village, I later discovered that the scene had reset itself. The local population—upright and unbloodied—were back in their original configurations: a still life of daily routine. And the six American soldiers had returned to their stealthy armed advance at the edge of the village. I searched their pewter faces, but none of them resembled my father anymore.

Had the diorama fulfilled its purpose? Or would the cycle repeat itself? I didn't want to find out.

I dismantled the whole thing, carried the pieces out to the garage, and reassembled it there. All except for the figurines of the American soldiers, which I sealed inside Dad's old metal tackle box. After placing a cinder block on the rust-speckled lid, I shoved the makeshift tomb under the workbench, back against the wall. Periodically, I go out to the garage and check that the cinder block remains in place. Then, lifting a corner of the tarp I draped over the diorama, I make sure the locals are still going peacefully about their daily lives.

I want that for myself, too: peaceful days. I want to be done with nursing my anxieties. And I want to see, in Leslie's eyes, a continued shift from murky grief to bright contentment. Is there an equinox for healing? Is the season drawing near?

All I can do is keep pushing forward, keep creating opportunities for happiness. With the diorama out of the way, I transformed my old bedroom into a rec room, with a card table for laying out jigsaw puzzles and playing board games, along with a vintage Evel Knievel pinball machine I found on eBay. Leslie owns the high score.

After my daydreamy minute of rest, I grab a bag of manure. The pungent odor catches at the back of my throat. I mix the manure with the loamy dirt, per Leslie's tutelage. She removes the sapling from the pot and sets it in the hole. Then we stake the baby tree in place so it won't topple over.

"Hard to imagine this little guy growing up to be a real tree," I say.

"Oh, I know it." Leslie shakes her head, affectionately it seems. "But I've watched it happen often enough."

I smile at the simple beauty of this moment. There's nothing I'd rather be doing right now, no one I'd rather be with. I must have once felt this same way about Sheila, but it's been so long now, and with enough rotten shit intervening, that I can no longer access that feeling. I'm just thankful the experience has found me again.

I stand and sigh. Before me, the denuded field awaits. We now have five saplings planted in the nascent citrus grove. The rest is bare earth and holes.

Acknowledgments

The author wishes to thank the following journals, where certain stories have been previously published:

"The Lioness" (*Thin Air Magazine*)

"A System of Dares" (*Stoneboat*)

"Clean Mojave Light" (*Whiskey Island*)

"Beyond the Gatehouse" (*Bluestem*)

"There Is a Tunnel" (*Tahoma Literary Review*)

* * *

I want to start by thanking everyone at Cornerstone Press for their care and enthusiasm for this collection, with special appreciation for Dr. Ross K. Tangedal for accepting my manuscript and for shepherding the work to publication, Eva Nielsen for her sharp editorial skills and for arranging the order of the pieces in the collection, Samantha Bjork for her gorgeous cover design, and for handling the nitty-gritty work of media and sales with Sophie McPherson, Madison Schultz, and Autumn Vine. It's been wonderful working with you all.

Thank you to Natalie Serber and Jon Raymond, whose workshops at the Attic Institute in the 2010s, made me a better writer.

Thank you to the 2023 members of my writing group, the Guttery. Tola Molotkov, Brittney Corrigan, Jackleen de la Harpe, Jennifer Brennock, and Lauren Fulton provided invaluable feedback and helped shape this collection's novella, "Orange Valley, White Valley."

I'm eternally grateful to Annie Bloom's Books, which has been so much more than a workplace for me these past twenty-five years. A special thanks to the store's founder, Bobby Tichenor, who passed away in 2024. Her love of literature has long inspired me, along with an entire community of readers.

A special thanks to my mother, Gaynl, to whom this book is dedicated. She raised me in the West and fostered my love of stories.

Most of all, thank you, Liz. For everything.

MICHAEL KEEFE is the author of *All Her Loved Ones, Encoded* (2024). Born and raised in the West, he is the Events Coordinator and Publicist at Annie Bloom's Books, an independent bookstore in Portland, Oregon, where he lives with his wife, the author Liz Prato, and their two cats.

www.ingramcontent.com/pod-product-compliance
Lightning Source LLC
Chambersburg PA
CBHW031049310726
48969CB00007B/2193